Dylan always moved fast...

With a startled cry, Cassie tumbled. He grabbed her, all his firefighter training and instincts kicking in before conscious thought. He tossed her to the bed, his own momentum carrying him in the same direction.

They fell to the bed. She somehow ended up underneath him.

He glanced down into her face, surprise and shock registering. Then he noticed that she was warm and soft beneath him and all the attraction he'd been pretending he didn't feel roared to the surface.

He leaned down. When he kissed her he felt the moment their lips touched that it had been inevitable from the second he'd walked into her house.

When she started to move against him, he felt his body harden in all the right places.

He wanted so much and he wanted it all now, but dimly an alarm began to ring as his mind finally caught up to the situation.

What the hell was he doing? He was supposed to be fixing up this woman's house.

And *not* jumping her luscious bones....

Blaze®

Dear Reader,

Sometimes a hero jumps off the page and seduces you. That happened to me with Dylan Cross. My gorgeous firefighter is brave to the point of recklessness, he's funny and he's got a heart of gold. How could I not fall in love with him? It wasn't easy giving him up to Cassie, a marine biologist whose element is water as much as his is fire. But don't worry. I made Cassie work for him!

I hope you enjoy the final book in the Last Bachelor Standing trilogy as much as I have enjoyed writing it.

I love to hear from readers, so please come visit me at www.nancywarren.net.

Happy reading,

Nancy Warren

Nancy Warren

Final Score

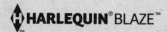
HARLEQUIN® BLAZE™

Recycling programs
for this product may
not exist in your area.

ISBN-13: 978-0-373-79806-3

FINAL SCORE

Copyright © 2014 by Nancy Warren

Printed in U.S.A.

ABOUT THE AUTHOR

USA TODAY bestselling author Nancy Warren lives in the Pacific Northwest, where her hobbies include skiing, hiking and snowshoeing. She's the author of more than thirty novels and novellas for Harlequin and has won numerous awards. Visit her website at www.nancywarren.net for news on upcoming titles.

Books by Nancy Warren

HARLEQUIN BLAZE
209—PRIVATE RELATIONS
275—INDULGE
389—FRENCH KISSING
452—UNDER THE INFLUENCE
502—POWER PLAY
526—TOO HOT TO HANDLE
553—MY FAKE FIANCÉE
569—THE EX FACTOR
597—FACE-OFF
706—JUST ONE NIGHT
785—GAME ON*
793—BREAKAWAY*

*Last Bachelor Standing

Cosmo Red-Hot Reads from Harlequin
HER VALENTINE FANTASY

Other titles by this author available in ebook format.

To get the inside scoop on Harlequin Blaze and its talented writers, be sure to check out blazeauthors.com.

This is for Viv Kefford, a dear friend, with thanks.

1

EVEN INSIDE HIS bunker gear, firefighter Dylan Cross could feel the heat from the burning house. Water cannoning from the big hoses made almost as much noise as the angry growl of the flames eating at the bungalow in a poorer section of Hunter, Washington.

There'd be a lot of mopping up to do, and not much of this old place would be saved, but the neighboring houses were unscathed, so that was something.

Even after ten years as a firefighter Dylan was still amazed at how alive each fire was, how a blaze had its own personality. Some were unpredictable drama queens, others quiet and stealthy as they ate through property, their smoky breath silently killing anyone unlucky enough to be sleeping without a smoke detector in the house.

It was getting on to 1:00 a.m. A few civilians in bathrobes and hastily donned clothes stood in clusters watching the fire. A dog nosed forward to sniff and quickly pulled back when a blast of flame shot out a window.

An ancient Ford screeched to a halt at the curb beside where Dylan stood and a young woman got out.

She had a six-pack of beer under her arm, and from the glazed eyes she was already under the influence of something. She stood and stared at the burning building, then started to glance around, increasingly agitated. "Terry? Terry!" She screamed the name over and over. Then she grabbed Dylan's arm. "He's in there. Terry's still in there."

Shit. "Where?" He tried to steady her. "Where is Terry?"

She pointed at the lower windows as though he were stupid. "In there. In the basement apartment."

He glanced up to find his captain, Len Butcher, striding over, shaking his head. But Dylan was already on the move. He grabbed an ax, ran around to the back of the house and found the door to the basement none of them had known existed. Damn it, the neighbors had said that the owners were away. Nobody had mentioned an apartment.

He didn't need the ax. He found that the door opened when he turned the knob. He did and was about to enter when his captain yelled. "Pull back! Damn it, Cross. Too dangerous. Pull back."

He registered the words, but only through the buzzing of adrenaline. Somebody inside. Had to get them out.

Dylan pushed in. Where the smoke was thick and the growl of the fire was much louder. To his left, a kitchen, on the right, squalid living quarters with the remains of a collection of plants. The bedroom was behind the living area, thick with smoke, and he could barely make out the hump in the bed. He ran forward, knowing time was running out. He could feel the tremble as the house succumbed. Inside his suit, sweat pooled.

He shook the limp man. No response. He reached

into the bed, hauled the guy up. Luckily, he was skin and bones and didn't weigh much. Dylan humped him over his shoulder and staggered back the way he'd come.

He almost made it.

He could make out the doorway, the way he'd come in, but as he ran for it, the ceiling caved in on them. It was like a fireworks display, all spark and sizzle. As he fell, he pitched forward, trying to throw the unconscious man out the door.

Then something hit him and he blacked out.

"YOU WENT AGAINST my direct order," Len Butcher yelled at him a week later when the doctor said he could return to work. Len had an unfortunate face. It was as if someone had crossed a bulldog with a baked potato. The result wasn't happy. His face was broad and dark-skinned, with that mash of nose in the middle just begging for a pat of butter and sour cream. "I had to risk two other firefighters to go in after you. You could have all been killed."

Dylan didn't bother defending himself. Terry was alive. Okay, he was a drug user and small-time dealer whose illegal power-sucking grow op had caused the fire, but Dylan felt that he should get some credit for saving the guy's life.

Len obviously didn't agree. "I don't have any room on my team for a hero with a death wish," he stormed, so red in the face he looked in danger of spontaneous combustion. "Do you understand me?"

"Yes, sir."

"You damn near were killed." Dylan understood that part of his anger was worry. "You're rash, a daredevil. You got away with a concussion and some bruises this time. It's a warning. And if that's not enough of one,

I'm giving you another." He raised his thick forefinger and shook it in Dylan's face. "I want you to take a couple of months and think about your future."

At this point Dylan dropped the hangdog act and glared at his captain. "A couple of months? I'm fine. Ready to go back to work."

"You had a concussion. You don't come back until I say you do. And I say you're on leave until further notice."

"But—"

"I mean it, Cross. Take some time. Figure out why you disobeyed my orders and how you'd feel if the two guys who went in to haul your ass out of there were in the morgue right now." He put up a hand before Dylan could protest. "Could have ended that way and you know it."

"But what the hell am I supposed to do for two months?"

"I don't know. And I don't care. Take up yoga, basket weaving, something quiet that won't get you killed. But stay out of trouble."

"But—"

"I swear, I hear one sniff about you doing some crazy-ass stunt and risking your life and you're off my team." He jerked a thumb toward the door. "Out."

CASSIE PRICE WAS in way over her head. Way, way, way over, she realized ruefully as she walked through the empty rooms of her new home.

Between them, her financial advisor, her parents and her real-estate agent had convinced her that buying a house in Hunter, Washington, was a great investment. The houses in her price range varied from tiny, boring new builds to older fixer-uppers with good bones. She'd bought the latter, although now, as she walked over brown shag carpet and peered at the harvest-gold appliances in the kitchen, she wondered about those bones, and if she hadn't in fact bought herself a hopeless dump.

The neighborhood was old and established and the homes in it were solidly built, she'd been told. And she could read decorating magazines and watch home-improvement shows like everybody else and see the potential in the hardwood floors hidden under the awful rugs, and sure, the kitchen would be fantastic with new appliances, cabinets, flooring and lighting.

Even the main bathroom would be a showpiece once she replaced the turquoise bathtub and sink and the vinyl flooring.

Her trouble was that she wasn't one of those handy types who could whip an old home into a showplace in a half-hour show, with plenty of time to spare for commercial breaks. She was a busy professional with zero skills and a limited budget. She couldn't afford a fancy home renovator.

As she walked from room to room, her distress grew.

Buyer's remorse? There had to be a stronger term for what she was suffering. *Buyer's panic* might be closer.

What had she done?

"What have I done?" She echoed the words when she joined her good friend and positive-thinking guru, Serena Long, and Serena's fiancé, Adam Shawnigan, for dinner at a local Greek restaurant, after touring the pair around her new-to-her house.

She speared a chunk of feta cheese and a tomato wedge from her salad.

Serena was a well-known performance coach. She and Cassie had first met a couple of years ago when Serena gave a workshop at the aquarium where Cassie worked as director of community outreach. Cassie had facilitated the workshop and they'd become friends almost immediately. Now Serena smiled that radiant smile of hers and said, "You bought a house. When it's renovated it will be a wonderful home. And a good investment."

"It's getting from here to renovated that seems to be the issue," Cassie said, shoving the food in her mouth and crunching down fiercely. "I need a miracle."

Adam chuckled. "You don't need a miracle. All you need is a decent handyman. A lot of the work in your home is cosmetic and grunt labor. You get a professional plumber and electrician for the tricky stuff, and then somebody like me who is handy and likes renovation projects can do the rest."

"Are you available?" she asked Adam sweetly.

Even though she'd said the words sarcastically, she knew he'd have helped her if he could. Adam was renovating his own house, the old cottage that he and Serena planned to live in when they got married in a few weeks.

"You know I would if I had the time," he said. Then she watched as he paused in the act of raising his water glass to his mouth. He put the glass back down and said, "But I think I know somebody who might be available."

She knew Adam was a perfectionist. He wouldn't recommend anyone who didn't meet his own rigorous standards, so a feeling of hope began to bloom. "Are you serious? Who?"

Serena turned to Adam. "Are you thinking what I'm thinking?"

"I usually am."

Cassie had found that this happened a lot with Serena and Adam. They had the whole married-speak thing going and they weren't even married yet. She waited,

knowing they'd fill her in when they'd finished tele-
pathically communing with each other.

Sure enough, Serena sat for a moment and then nodded. "I agree. It's a very good idea. Solves both their
problems."

Adam turned back to Cassie. "I happen to know a
very handy guy who suddenly has a couple of months
of free time and really, really needs a project. Let me
tell you about my good friend Dylan Cross."

She listened as Adam described his firefighter friend
Dylan, who'd apparently dragged the operator of an illegal grow op from a burning house, almost getting
himself killed in the process, and then was put on suspension for ignoring his captain's orders. She could see
how it might be aggravating to have a heroic deed like
that go unappreciated. She could also see that he might
be a problem.

"This Dylan Cross is in trouble because he ignored
his boss's orders." She looked from Adam to Serena.
"How do I know he won't ignore my orders when he's
working on my house?"

"It's simple," Adam said, leaning forward and lowering his voice. "We need Dylan at the upcoming championship hockey game for Badges on Ice. If he loses
his job, we lose a valuable right wing. So if you have
any problem with Dylan, even the tiniest hint of trouble, you will call me, and I and our teammate Max
will be all over him." She'd met Max Varo a couple of
times and the billionaire entrepreneur always intimidated her a little.

Cassie leaned back and crossed her arms over her
chest. "So basically what you're saying is you want me
to babysit a guy who has problems with impulse control?"

"He's a good guy, honestly. Dylan, Max and me, we go way back. Our moms were all friends and we played together as little kids, went through school, joined all the same teams. I know Dylan Cross through and through. Yes, he's a little rash, but if I was in any kind of trouble I'd want him to have my back."

She knew Adam wouldn't use words like that lightly. An outstanding police officer himself, Adam mostly associated with law-and-order types. People of integrity. If he vouched for this Dylan Cross, then she was willing to take a chance.

Besides, she did really, really need a handyman.

But she wasn't going to be a pushover, either. She gave Adam the steely-eyed gaze that she used if a school kid wasn't behaving during a visit to the aquarium. "I'll make a deal with you. I will babysit your boy. But you are personally in charge of making sure he does an excellent job, and that he sticks to a tight budget."

Adam grinned at her. "You two are going to get on like a house on fire. So to speak."

She smacked his hand. "Is there anything else I need to know?"

It was Serena who spoke. "One thing that might be good to know." She sent Cassie a woman-to-woman look. "He's Mr. June. In the charity firefighter calendar." She waved a hand in front of her face as though she were perspiring. "You have to check him out."

2

SATURDAY MORNINGS USED to be Cassie's favorite time of the entire week. Ahh, those lazy Saturday mornings when she could take a cup of tea back to bed with her, download something new on her e-reader or pick an old favorite from her crowded bookshelves. Then she'd settle back against the pillows and read. She'd get up when she felt like it and then worry about organizing her day.

Those Saturday mornings were over.

Now when she opened her eyes on the first weekend in her new home, she didn't see the familiar walls of her rental-apartment bedroom, with her art hanging and bookcases begging to be raided. Instead she saw ugly pink walls and packing boxes that she wouldn't unpack until the room was painted. Her head vibrated with the mental to-do list that seemed longer than her future. And a lot more frightening.

But at least Adam's friend Dylan was coming by today to take a look at the place and give her an estimate on what he could do for her and how much it would cost.

She really hoped that Adam was right and his buddy, the temporarily unemployed firefighter, would be both competent and reasonably priced.

And how did she feel about a man who was suspended from his regular job because he'd ignored his boss's orders? She wondered as she brewed tea and made toast, trying to ignore the harvest-gold appliances and chipped mint-green countertops as she did so. What if he ignored her instructions?

Adam maintained that Dylan had put saving a life ahead of bureaucracy, but still, you had to wonder.

While she ate breakfast, she scanned this week's flyers from local hardware stores and big-box DIY places and wondered, not for the first time, if she'd made a terrible mistake. When she'd found out her grandmother had left her a little money, her parents had both encouraged her to buy her own place. "You know renting is throwing money down the drain," her mom had insisted.

"We've always made money on our houses," her father, the accountant, had added.

But her father was handy. And lived far away in California. The two of them had bonded not over carpentry but over scuba diving, a passion that had led to her current career.

It wasn't that she didn't want a house. She did, of course, and she believed her parents and her financial advisor and the real-estate agent when they'd said that it was a good long-term investment. She imagined what her three-bedroom home could look like and knew it could be warm and beautiful. Even the neglected garden could shine with some love and attention.

If she knew the first thing about gardening.

When the doorbell rang later that day, she was almost ready to shove the For Sale sign back in front of the house.

She opened the door.

And the best-looking man she'd ever seen—who

wasn't staring back at her from a movie screen, TV set or a billboard—stood there. "Hi, I'm Dylan," he said, all sexy and hot with his tousled hair that looked as though he'd only just gotten out of bed after leaving a woman or two very happy. His eyes were the kind of blue that reminded her of the seas she loved to dive in. His teeth were white and even and he was tall. His clothes might be scruffy but nothing could downplay the exquisite tone of his body.

She actually had to blink and give her overloaded senses a moment. When she opened her eyes he was still there and still as spectacular. Of course, she should have realized that he wasn't your run-of-the-mill kind of man when Serena had mentioned he was Mr. June and fanned her face. Serena was engaged to Adam Shawnigan, who wasn't exactly dogmeat to look at. If she was getting gooey over another guy's appearance—well, he'd look like this man.

"Cassie," she managed when she could form a word. "Come on in." Then she saw the toolbox. "Oh, you brought tools." She'd imagined this would be a preliminary session where he'd look around the house then go home and prepare a budget and maybe give her a supply list.

He shrugged. "Adam said you want to get started right away and personally, I hate wasting time."

She had her first inkling that they were going to get on just fine.

"Unless you take one look at this place and run screaming out again." She sighed. "There's a lot of work here."

Dylan stepped in around her and began to touch and poke at and inspect things. She'd planned to give him a tour and point out the areas she most wanted tackled, but he seemed to have his own agenda. Fascinated, she followed him. He didn't take notes, merely nodded and muttered as he pulled on the banister (which was solid, that got a nod), opened a kitchen cabinet (headshake and muttering), then glanced around. "You'll want a separate electric panel up here in the kitchen. For that you'll need a licensed electrician. I can recommend one."

"Thanks."

"He can also change that fluorescent lighting to something from this century."

Without missing a thing he was zeroing in on her list of absolute must-haves.

He dropped to his knees and pulled at a corner of the kitchen flooring. That got a groan.

But when they got to the living room and he pulled up a corner of the awful shag rug, he not only nodded, he traced the inlaid wood pattern with a finger. "You can't buy this kind of workmanship anymore."

Upstairs, he bounced on the floor, then walked into the bathroom and said, "Wow." He continued through each of the three bedrooms, then took her all the way down to the basement and walked around. When they got back up to the main level he stood once more in the living room and turned slowly around.

"You know," Dylan said, "this place has great potential."

"Oh, how I am beginning to hate that word."

When he grinned at her she almost forgot to breathe. "Don't worry. We'll get her so she's better than new. First, I have to warn you, things will get worse. Messy and noisy and destructive. But then things will get a lot better, and fast."

She nodded. "Define *fast*."

He had a confidence about him that made her feel

everything would be all right. "A month from now you won't recognize the place. Two months from now, you'll have forgotten it ever looked this bad."

"I can't imagine I'll ever forget." She'd better take lots of pictures along the way.

"Now, Adam says you're on a budget, so here's what I propose. We tackle the absolute worst things that you can't live with and then go from there. Absolute worst for me would be bathroom, then kitchen. It's easy and not very expensive to strip out all the carpets and refinish the hardwood floors. Big bang for your buck. If you want to save money, you have to help. What can you do?"

When he turned those gorgeous blue eyes on her, she tried to come up with something, some previously undiscovered handy-person trait. "I can choose the fixtures and colors and things."

"Good. Can you paint?"

"Uh, I guess so. How hard can it be?"

"That's the attitude. I'll show you a few tricks. Paint makes a huge difference and it's relatively cheap."

"Have you done many renovations?"

"Sure. Didn't Adam tell you? I buy and fix up houses and then sell them. It's a hobby of mine. I also take on projects for other people when I'm off duty." He frowned. "At the moment I have some extra time." There was an awkward pause. "Adam probably told you."

"Yeah."

"My unexpected time off is bad news for me, but good news for you."

She really hoped that was true.

Within half an hour of him walking in the door, not

only had she hired him, but Cassie already had him working in her house.

And she knew within another half an hour that she hadn't made a mistake. He'd gotten right on his cell phone and lined up a plumber and an electrician to give quotes on the job. Then he said, "I could have that carpet out of here today. What do you think?"

She was nodding crazily before she got to the word *yes*.

"It's going to make a big difference right away."

She began to feel less overwhelmed. It was as though she had a team now. Even if it was only her and one man. At least the one man seemed to have the energy of three.

"While I'm taking care of that, you'll need to pick your bathroom fixtures and kitchen cabinets. Appliances, too, sooner rather than later."

"I've got some ideas already. I've been filing clippings and pictures." She was so unsure and he must have heard the hesitation in her tone.

"Want me to take a look? I've done a lot of this stuff."

"Would you?"

"Sure."

She had several files of material, pictures she'd torn from magazines, ideas she'd printed off the internet and of course the ads from the flyers that appeared constantly in her mailbox.

"I like this kitchen," he said after flipping through her idea file. "You could replicate the cabinets using Ikea or Home Depot stock. I've got a buddy who can get you those countertops. For the flooring, do you really want that tile?"

"What's wrong with it?"

He pointed to the tile in the photo and she noticed

that his finger was burn scarred. "See those ridges? It's going to make the floor hard to keep clean. And if you drop anything, it's going to shatter."

"What do you suggest?"

"I'd go with cork. I think it suits your look, and it's environmentally friendly and easy to clean."

"Thanks. I'll think about it."

He flipped through some more of her stash and stopped. "Yes!" He said it with such enthusiasm she wondered what he was looking at. It was a magazine makeover from a bathroom like hers to a modern one that looked like a spa. "I was going to ease you into this idea, but you're way ahead of me. If you move the bathtub so it's across the back wall under the window, that gets rid of the ugly alleyway. You've probably got room for a stand-alone shower, too, if you go with a smaller vanity."

"Really?" She was as enthusiastic as he was. "I could have this?"

"Absolutely. It will cost a little more since you're moving plumbing, but it's so worth it. We'll save money in other places."

She nodded. "Deal."

"Okay, then. You start shopping, and I'll start pulling out carpet."

As she got busy, her initial excitement about buying this house resurfaced. She'd let herself become overwhelmed, she realized. All she had to do was take the renovation one step at a time.

She had a feeling that hiring Dylan had been an excellent first step.

He was soon on his hands and knees pulling up the ugly carpet from the living and dining rooms. Fortunately, he was wearing a dust mask, because she could see billows of old dirt flying into the air whenever he pulled a new piece up. He cut and rolled the rug into sections and then hefted them all out to the truck he'd parked in her driveway.

Then he came back and began removing the nail board tacked around the edges of the floor.

The transformation was amazing—no more ugly shag.

The floors weren't perfect—there were a few paint splotches and all those nail holes—but they'd been covered with carpet for so long that they were barely worn.

"This looks so much better," she said, hearing her voice echo in the empty room. "And it doesn't smell so dusty. I don't even want to think about what was in that carpet."

He glanced up at her from his position, kneeling on the floor and said, "I won't sand them yet. We'll get most of the dirty stuff done first. But I like the impact getting rid of that old carpet makes. You start to see the possibilities." He leaned right back onto his heels and glanced at her thoughtfully. "That's what you bought, after all."

She stared right back at him. "I did. I bought myself a houseful of possibilities."

3

DYLAN LIKED THIS HOUSE. It was the kind of place he might have bought himself if he'd been looking for a project. Instead, it was nice to work for somebody else for a change, not be responsible for all of it, not live in the mess.

He hadn't been sure how Cassie would manage living in a construction zone. It wasn't for everyone. But after that first day, when she'd seemed as though she thought she'd made a terrible mistake, she'd come on board. He thought her ideas were good and she was smart enough to take advantage of his experience. She was easy on the eyes, too, he mused as he hefted the butt-ugly vanity out of the main bathroom and set it beside the even uglier turquoise sink.

He stretched out his back, knowing his next task was to remove the old bathtub. That old beast had hulked in that spot for fifty years or so—he didn't figure it was coming out without a fight.

Cassie wouldn't be home from work for an hour or two, so the noise and occasional swearing weren't going to bother her. He had the place to himself. The bathroom window was wide open to let in the fresh air of a bright spring day. After this, he promised himself, he'd sit outside with a soda and enjoy the sunshine for a few minutes.

As he prepared to do battle with the tub, he heard what sounded like a baby crying.

He paused, thinking the noise had been awfully close, almost as if there was a baby inside the house. He stopped, listened carefully and heard the sad, plaintive cry again.

Dylan had been a firefighter too long to ignore any sound of distress. He jogged quickly through the house but no one was there.

Outside he ran. No one in the front. Around to the back. He heard the sound again. Louder now, and coming from above him.

Shading his eyes with his hand, he looked up. The tree was an old one, gnarled and solid, the cedar standing probably fifty feet tall. And halfway up a kitten was crying its heart out.

"Oh, no," he said to himself. To the kitten he tried the positive approach. "Come on, kitty. You got up there. You can come down."

The reply was an even more pathetic howl of distress.

He glanced around as though a neighbor might be outside, maybe with a ladder. But on a sunny Monday afternoon, Dylan seemed to be the only one around.

He tried calling to the cat again. No dice.

Then he ran into Cassie's kitchen and found a can of tuna in her cupboards. He dug through her kitchen drawer and pulled out a can opener. Took a nice chunk of tuna on a saucer out to the cat to try and lure it out of the tree.

The cat only sounded more woebegone than ever.

At this point, Dylan had to accept the kitten was stuck in that tree.

Glad none of his colleagues or friends was around to laugh at him for being such a cliché, he put the tuna on the ground, rubbed his hands on his filthy jeans and pulled himself up to the first branch of the tree.

He'd been climbing trees as long as he'd been walking. The first time he'd fallen out of one his mother had claimed he must have nine lives. Lately she'd been warning him that he'd used most of them up.

It was sort of fun to climb a tree at the age of thirty-five. And it was giving a good stretch to the muscles that had been bent over doing grunt work at the house.

When he drew closer, he saw that the cat was very young. And very scared.

"You're not going to scratch my eyes out, are you?" he asked when his face was level with the cat's. In answer, the animal butted its small head against his hand.

He chuckled. "Okay, then." He took a moment to scratch the kitten behind the ears until he heard it start to purr. Then, very gently, he scooped the small, warm body into one hand and lifted it toward his shoulder. A glimpse at the back end told him the animal was most likely a female. The cat caught right on and crawled up so she was hanging over his shoulder, digging in tight.

Dylan winced as tiny, sharp claws grabbed him through his thin T-shirt, but at least he had his hands free and the animal seemed to recognize that he was trying to save her.

"Going down," he said, as though he were an elevator operator.

He shimmied down the tree, talking softly to the cat the whole way. He swung down from the lowest branch. "Hang on tight, now," he said to his companion, and dropped down to the grass, one hand hanging onto his burden.

As he turned, he discovered he was no longer alone.

Cassie was standing in the backyard, staring at him. Obviously home early from work. And she'd brought her friend, Adam's fiancée, Serena, with her.

"What on earth?" Cassie blinked at him.

He felt suddenly like a kid caught playing hooky. Instead of working on her house, she'd caught him climbing trees. He could feel bits of leaves in his hair, his clothes were even more filthy than they'd been earlier and he had a kitten hanging over his shoulder, claws so far into him he didn't think she was ever letting go.

He decided to work on the most important thing first—getting the kitten disengaged from his flesh. With as much dignity as he could muster, he said to Cassie, "Could you pass me that tuna?"

The two women exchanged a glance that had a lot of suppressed humor in it, and he strongly suspected there was a certain gender mocking going on. Not that he could prove it, since neither of them said anything. Cassie picked up the saucer with the chunk of tuna on it and passed it over.

"Thank you." He turned his back so the kitten's head would face her. "Maybe you could try feeding the cat so she gets her claws out of my skin."

"Ouch," she said.

Then he heard her speak softly to the kitten. "It's okay. I've got some yummy tuna for you, but you have to let go of Dylan first." It was the sort of voice a mom would use with a toddler, but it worked fine. Or the smell of tuna did. He felt the claws release and then the small, warm body was lifted from his shoulder. When he turned around, the cat was already on the ground, happily chowing down.

He rubbed his chest with his knuckles and frowned at his new boss, who was looking distractingly hot in a skirt and heels that showed off shapely legs. "Don't you know cats need time to get used to a new home? You can't just let them out and leave them."

Her eyes widened in surprise and he figured she'd made the dumb mistake of thinking that because she'd moved the cat she would settle right in. Big mistake. She was lucky the feline hadn't hiked back to wherever she'd lived before.

"Your cat doesn't even have a collar. What if she had wandered? Could have got lost." The cat looked up from its empty plate then and meowed, as though in full agreement.

Cassie knelt down and patted the kitten's head. She was obviously fond of her housemate.

Which made him continue, "I'm surprised you wouldn't be a better pet owner, seeing as you work at the aquarium."

She looked up at him, which made her eyes seem big. "I would if I owned a pet. But I don't."

He began to feel incredibly foolish. "You mean—"

"This isn't my cat."

He found two pairs of large eyes regarding him. "I, ah, I'm going to rip that tub out of the bathroom now," he said, backing away.

AFTER DYLAN DISAPPEARED into the house, Cassie rose with the kitten in her arms. She looked at Serena and they both stifled giggles. Serena said, "Did we just witness a fireman rescuing a kitten from a tree?"

"Yep. And he looked awfully good doing it."

"He looks good doing just about anything," Serena agreed. "Too bad he can't grow up."

"What do you mean?"

"Did I tell you about Last Bachelor Standing?"

"I don't think so. I'd have remembered."

Serena shook her head. "Well, when the three boys—and I do mean *boys*—Adam, Dylan and Max, were all celebrating Adam's thirty-fifth birthday back in February, every one of them was still single. They challenged each other to one of their stupid contests. They've known each other forever and have this strange compulsion to set up bets. This one was who would be the last bachelor standing."

"You've got to be joking."

Serena shook her head once more.

"Obviously, Adam didn't win," Cassie said, pointing to Serena's engagement ring.

A purely feminine smile was her response. "No. He did not. Then Max went to Alaska and fell for that bush pilot who, let's just say, took him down in flames."

"Which leaves Dylan."

"Yep. Undisputed winner of the contest, which I like to call Last Guy to Grow Up."

Cassie could hear banging and sawing coming from the bathroom so she knew they couldn't be overheard. "Is he proud of this so-called accomplishment?"

"He brags about it every time the guys get together."

She glanced up at the bathroom window. "Sometimes I think it's a wonder our species survives."

"Speaking of survival," Serena said, regarding the rescue cat, "what are you going to do about this little stray?"

The kitten was purring loudly in her arms, but she

could feel that the animal was skin and bone. "I guess I'll meet my new neighbors, see if anyone claims it."

"It might belong to the last people who lived here. Sometimes cats find their way home."

Cassie dumped the rest of the can of tuna into the saucer. Then she said to Serena, "Come on in. I'll show you the progress so far, as promised. And you can help me choose paint colors."

"As promised. Where do you want to start?"

"My bedroom. I cannot stand waking up every morning surrounded by walls the color of already chewed bubblegum."

"Let's go."

But first she had to stop and admire the hardwood floors. "These are going to be so beautiful when they're refinished."

"I know. I can't believe the difference already."

As they walked upstairs she described the bedroom of her imagination. "I want something very feminine. I work with fish and marine mammals and scientists all day. I want my bedroom to be a woman's retreat."

They entered the room and she immediately saw what she wanted. "I've seen a yellow-and-blue duvet cover that I love, and I'll have chintz cushions in the window seat in a coordinating fabric."

Serena nodded. "The window seat really is pretty, with that view out into the garden. I love those multi-paned windows. So country cottage."

"I think that window seat might have sold me this house," she admitted.

"What about a chandelier for a light fixture?" The one crouching over a single lightbulb in the ceiling was a square of etched glass that must have been ugly even in the '60s.

"Ooh, I like it. And I'm looking for an antique head-board. I haven't found one yet, but I'll know it when I see it."

"Nice. And you've got an en-suite bathroom, which is such a great feature."

"But what color for the walls?"

Serena took a few moments to walk right into the bedroom. She sat on the window seat. Looked into the room. "I am seeing a French blue. Something soft, but the color of lavender."

"Oh, that's perfect." Cassie picked up the fan of paint colors she'd bought to help her choose and began to flip. There were so many shades they made her eyes hurt, but Serena helped her and they finally decided on a color that both agreed would be wonderful. For the bathroom they decided on a darker shade of the same lavender color. The color would go well with the dark wood cabinet she'd scored for half price in a high-end decorating store that was changing its stock.

Cassie added two different colors of paint to her growing list of supplies to purchase, then added a chandelier because the idea pleased her so much. She knew that if she could get even this one room finished, she'd feel more settled.

When she turned to leave she found that the cat had followed them and had settled herself on the window seat, nestled among the cushions she'd put there temporarily.

Since she was sound asleep after her ordeal in the tree, Cassie decided to leave her to sleep.

Tomorrow she'd find her home. And if she turned out to be a stray, she supposed she'd have to find the nearest animal shelter.

A ray of late-afternoon sun shone on the kitten's tortoiseshell coat and as she dreamed, her whiskers twitched.

SERENA ALSO HAD some good ideas for other rooms, including sophisticated neutrals for the main downstairs rooms. When Cassie had jotted down a list of colors, she offered Serena a drink, but her friend shook her head. "Can't. I've got to run. I've got an appointment to view a hotel ballroom for the wedding reception." She flapped a hand to her chest and her engagement ring flashed. "Booking a wedding without a year's lead time is crazy. Everything decent is already booked." She sighed. "Fortunately, I have connections and I'm very persuasive."

"If it was me, I'd want to get married outside."

"Me, too. And good luck with that. My advice? When you get married, give yourself plenty of planning time."

"I should probably start by actually going out on a date."

Serena nodded. She understood. In the past they'd bonded over being single professional women and laughed about their bad dates. Now Serena had found the love of her life. Cassie still seemed to be stuck in single mode.

"I can't believe I'm getting married," Serena suddenly said, looking uncertain.

"I can. It suits you." It did, too. Serena had always possessed the most amazing confidence but now that she'd found love there was a deeper calmness that hadn't been there before. Perhaps it was contentment.

After Serena left, Cassie walked toward the main-floor bathroom—soon to be a magazine-inspired transformation—to check on progress. And found the cat seeming to do the same. She sat, tail curled around her paws, watching Dylan manhandle the tub. He was sweating and his muscles bulged. A wave of lust, as unexpected as it was unwelcome, crashed over Cassie as she watched him.

"Can I help?" she asked.

"I'll get a buddy to help me heft the tub out of here," he grunted.

"I can do it," she insisted. "Give me two seconds to change my clothes."

"It's heavy," he warned.

"I heft all the time at work."

In not much more than two seconds she'd shoved herself into a pair of old jeans and a T-shirt she'd gotten somewhere for free and should never have accepted.

"Take the other pair of work gloves from my toolbox," he said, "and let me know if it's too heavy."

The tub was heavy, all right, but she worked out, and as a diver she was used to carrying heavy equipment. She'd manage.

The tub was not only ugly and heavy but the edges she had to hold dug into her hands even through the gloves. No way could she simply drop it halfway to the door, so she gritted her teeth, tightened every core muscle she could locate and slowly, step by step, they got the beast down the hall then out the front door. He'd already put down the back of his truck, so they walked it right over and wedged and heaved until the hulk of metal humped in the truck bed like a beached gray whale.

The cat followed them, watching the operation with interest.

"You're stronger than you look," Dylan said, wiping

a bead of sweat from his forehead with the back of his hand, running his gaze down her body in a way that made her tingle.

"I—" She had no idea what to say. Their gazes connected and she felt that pull of attraction once more, stronger now that she suspected he felt it, too.

"Hi, there," a female voice called out, breaking the spell.

They both turned and a pleasant-looking woman in her forties stood at the edge of the drive, smiling. "I'm Lynette Peters. My family and I live next door." She indicated the white house on Cassie's right with a front yard full of blooming spring flowers. "Welcome to the neighborhood."

"Thank you," Cassie said, walking forward. She pulled the work glove from her right hand and shook hands. "I'm Cassie Price. I do have one question." She pointed to the cat sitting behind the truck licking one paw. "Do you know whose cat this is?"

The woman glanced down at the kitten and shook her head. "I don't recognize her and I know most of the pets around here. I'd say she's a stray. Poor little thing. People should get their cats spayed."

"I know. I was hoping she had a home. I guess I'll have to take her to the shelter. Maybe they can find her a home."

"Well, you let us know if you need anything, you or your husband."

"Oh," Cassie said, "Dylan's not my husband."

On his way back to the house, Dylan sent Lynette his lady-killer grin and said, "She just uses me for sex."

"Dylan!" She felt her cheeks warm, probably because she'd been lusting after him only a few minutes earlier. She turned back to Lynette. "He's joking. Of course we're not, uh, you know…"

Lynette watched Dylan saunter back to the house. "Then you must be crazy."

4

How could one silly, joking comment change everything? Cassie wondered as she walked back into the house and found Dylan carrying a rusted length of pipe down the hall toward her. She held the front door wide for him and as he passed she wondered what it would be like to enjoy a man only for sex. She'd never tried it before, but with Dylan, she could see the appeal. The lust wasn't all coming from her. She recognized the interest in his eyes.

Even without Serena's subtle warning earlier, she could tell Dylan was a player. There was something about a really sexy guy that said he knew exactly the impact he had on women. It wasn't his fault, she supposed—it must be hard to be that sexy and gorgeous and not end up a little full of yourself.

So she knew he was a player, and normally she was immune from such practiced charm. It was incredibly bad luck that Dylan should be the one to get to her. When they were spending so much time together.

She'd simply have to let him believe she was as immune to him as she wished she were.

It wasn't that she was in a hurry to settle down or

anything, but there was something wrong with considering getting involved in even the most casual way with a man who prided himself on being the last bachelor standing.

Over the first week they fell into a routine. He'd arrive in the morning before she left for work, and when she returned, he'd show her the day's progress, suggest her next task and often stay working with her.

When she protested that he was working too many hours, he shrugged. "I like to keep busy." She thought maybe working on her house prevented him from brooding over his job woes, and since she enjoyed working with him in the house—and the sooner her house was done, the better—she didn't argue.

When Saturday arrived, she wasn't a bit surprised to see him show up, his hair damp as though he'd just stepped out of the shower. Obviously misinterpreting the way she was staring at him, he said, "Sorry I'm a little late today. I always do a longer workout at the gym on the weekends."

Which told her that not only was he working out on top of the exhausting physical labor of a home renovation, but that he considered every day a workday. "I wish I had your energy," she said.

"I've gotta stay in shape for the championship hockey game," he told her, helping himself from the pot of coffee she'd made.

"Oh, right. Adam said something about an emergency-services league."

"Right. Play-offs in a few weeks. Our team, the Hunter Hurricanes, gets so close every year to winning, but this year that trophy is ours."

"Isn't this a charity event? To raise money for a good cause?"

"Sure it is. Doesn't mean we don't all go out there and play to win." Then he glanced up. "You should come and watch one of our games sometime."

It was the first time he'd suggested anything remotely unrelated to their project, and she was startled. And pleased. "Oh, thanks. I'd love to."

The kitten appeared, scampering on her little kitten legs to meow at Dylan's feet. He scooped the cat up so they were nose to nose. "How are you doing, Twinkletoes?"

A purr was the answer. He put the cat over his shoulder in a practiced way that she suspected happened a lot when she wasn't home. The cat hung there, purring with content, while Dylan drank more coffee.

He didn't mention that she still had the cat almost a week after they'd found it, so she felt she should explain. "I put a poster up around the neighborhood. I'm hoping someone claims her." She did not refer to the cat as Twinkletoes, feeling that naming a stray was a straight path to cat ownership. And right now she was still struggling with the home-ownership thing. She couldn't take on more responsibility. As cute as the kitten was.

"Any bites?"

"Nothing. I'll keep the cat a few more days and try and fatten her up a bit before taking her to the shelter."

He didn't answer. Merely walked back to the kitchen and placed the now empty mug in the sink.

"I'm filling the cracks and holes in my bedroom walls today, then I'll try my hand at painting." She figured if she screwed up on her bedroom, it wasn't too serious. Hopefully by the time she got to the downstairs main rooms she'd be a pro.

"I'm back in the bathroom. For the smallest room in the house, it's going to be one of the biggest time sucks."

She understood, and also knew how fantastic it was going to look when that bathroom was done. She'd chosen the fixtures with care. The tile, even the wall paint. He walked toward the bathroom, the cat hanging off him like a funky stole, and she headed for the stairs.

She got to work with her scraper, getting rid of some of the loose old paint and then filling in the nail holes and a few shallow cracks with filler. She kind of liked the mindless work. She put on NPR for a while and then found she wasn't listening, so she flipped to a music station.

"Cassie! Come here," Dylan yelled from the direction of the bathroom.

She dropped her paint scraper and ran to the bathroom, picturing him trapped under a heavy object or something, but when she got there she found him with hands on hips, admiring the latest layer of decorative wall covering he'd bared.

"This must be the original," he said.

She walked into the bathroom, immediately feeling the closeness of their two bodies brushing as they contemplated what had to have been the ultimate in bathroom decor back in the 1950s.

He put a friendly arm on her shoulder. "It's you."

The wallpaper was in blue and turquoise tones with splashes of gold. It showed a mermaid riding a dolphin. Or maybe a whale. Whoever had designed the paper wasn't a marine biologist. But she loved the whimsy of the busty mermaid with her long, flowing hair and rounded hips ending in a green tail that looked a lot like a slinky gown. She rode sidesaddle on her willing aquatic ride. "She's one sexy mermaid."

"You see? This was meant to be. You're a woman of the sea and this wallpaper is a sign that this is supposed to be your house."

She looked at him. "You really believe that?"

He shrugged. "Why not? Too bad we can't save more of it."

"She looks like you, too," he said, glancing at the buxom mermaid and back at Cassie. There was a warm, teasing light in his eyes that was hard to resist.

"You think I'd look good in scales?"

"I think you'd look good in anything." There was no denying, the man had some serious charm going on. Also, this space was small and he was so hot and it had been so long and… The moment lingered, his gaze on hers, a ripple of energy between them not unlike the ripple of the water's surface when a fin has fluttered by.

Oh, this was such a bad idea, she thought as her heart began to pound and he moved infinitesimally closer.

The shrill ringing of the phone brought her back to reality faster than a plunge into cold water. She backed away fast. "I should get that." She tucked her hair behind her ears in a nervous gesture she'd had since grade school.

His eyes tilted at the corners in wry amusement, maybe some disappointment. "You should." Then he turned back to his task of removing whimsical '50s mermaids from her walls and she ran to answer her landline.

"Hey, Dylan?" she yelled to him from the kitchen.

"Yeah?"

"The floor tile's in. I'm going to pick it up."

"Okay. Need a hand?"

Well, she did and she didn't. She figured the guys at the warehouse could schlep the tiles into her car and Dylan could help her unload them when she got back.

Which gave her an hour or so out on the road on her own to talk some sense into herself.

Besides, there was something so unsexy about a tile warehouse, maybe it would be the decorating equivalent of the cold shower she really needed right now.

"No. That's okay. Do you need anything while I'm out?"

There was a tiny pause. "No. I'm good." She heard him bang into something and swear, then he yelled, "Oh, no, wait. Can you get me some three-quarter-inch finishing nails?"

"Three-quarter-inch finishing nails."

"Yeah. And then I'm good."

No, you're not. You're bad. Badbadbadbadbad!

While she was heading to the warehouse, her cell phone rang. She answered on her Bluetooth. "Hello?"

"Hey, Cassie. It's Serena. What are you up to?"

"Going to pick up floor tiles, you?"

"Escaping to the gym. Adam decided he needed to install some sort of flashing over the window. A great deal of noise was involved."

"Yeah, Dylan's pulling my bathroom apart. Noise, dust—" *Sexual temptation of the hottest kind.*

"Don't you miss those Saturdays when you could go for brunch and maybe do a little shopping? Get your nails done?"

"Not only can I barely remember those days, I can't even afford them anymore. Everybody said a house was a good investment, but all I ever do is dump more money into it."

"I know. When I signed up for a Lowe's credit card I knew my days at the spa were over."

Since Serena was a very successful corporate coach with a bestselling leadership book, Cassie doubted this was completely true, but she appreciated the sympathy anyway.

"Did you find your chandelier yet?"

"Haven't even looked."

"I was in this little hole-in-the-wall antique and secondhand store and I found one that, to me, looks perfect. It's not too far past the tile warehouse. I'll grab a quick workout while you pick up your tiles and meet you there if you like."

"Oh," Cassie squealed. "Chandeliers are so much more interesting than three-quarter-inch finishing nails."

"That is so true." Serena gave her the directions and they agreed to meet at the store in an hour.

When she'd finished getting the tiles loaded into her car, she had time to get the finishing nails. Boring.

The paint store was beside the hardware place, so she pulled out her credit card one more time. The back of her car was fairly loaded by the time she'd finished, but she definitely had a chandelier-size space left.

Definitely.

And she knew Serena had excellent taste, so her hopes were high.

They faltered a little when Cassie found her way to Murphy's Antiques and Secondhand Finds. The store was in a plaza with a secondhand sports-equipment outlet and some kind of automotive place.

Nevertheless, she pushed her way into the store. A bell rang, and when she took a step inside she knew Serena hadn't steered her wrong. This was a store to browse in. Junk and treasure were jumbled together—old toys, clothing and books, Depression glass to Irish crystal to sterling silver and old tobacco tins. The lighting fixtures hung from the ceiling. An enormous brass wagon wheel with black lamps would have looked at home in the Munsters' house, and there were stained-glass lamps and a bright orange midcentury modern globe and—oh, that had to be it. A small chandelier, delicate and twinkly when the door opened and the breeze shivered through the crystals.

"What do you think?" Serena asked, coming up behind her.

Cassie turned to her and beamed. "It's perfect."

"I knew it."

"But it's on hold." She pointed at the big tag hanging from the fixture.

"I had them put it on hold. For you."

"Ha. Fantastic."

"How can I help you ladies?" a balding man with a large stomach hanging over his belt asked them.

"We'll take this chandelier," Serena said.

"Wait. How much is it?"

Serena put a hand on her arm. "It's a housewarming gift."

"No. You can't."

"I was going to buy it, but then I thought how awful if you hated it. There is nothing worse than being stuck with a gift you don't like. So I dragged you out of your way to approve of my taste before I made a fool of myself."

"As if you could."

Cassie hugged her friend quickly, knowing that Serena was as pleased to be giving her the chandelier as she was to receive it.

"I'm going to start painting the bedroom as soon as I get home," she said. "I'll make Dylan stop work on the bathroom and help me. I can't wait to get that room in shape. It's going to be so beautiful."

"The whole house is going to be beautiful. You wait."

While the store owner boxed the light up for them, they browsed, picking through old farm tools and vinyl records, a tray of pocket watches and boxes of linens. "My grandmother always used to smell like Joy," she said, picking up an old bottle of the French perfume. The bottle was empty, but there was an echo of scent that reminded her of her mother's mom, a wonderful woman who played piano and baked the best pies.

"My grandmother smelled like this," Serena said, picking up an old can with "Player's Tobacco" written on it.

They had such different backgrounds it was amazing they'd become friends. Serena rarely talked about her past, but through passing comments like this one, Cassie knew it had been rough. Serena had dragged herself up from the gutter to become one of the most successful women in Cassie's circle, while Cassie had two parents who loved her, were still married and still called each other sweetheart. How did she get so lucky?

Of course, Serena was getting married to one of the best men on the planet, while Cassie had celebrated her thirtieth birthday still single. Her present to herself had been a three-bedroom house she'd have trouble filling.

Unless she took in a lot more stray cats.

5

THEY CARRIED THE chandelier out to the car, fitting it nicely in the space Cassie had set aside. Then Serena said, "Max is flying in to play hockey with the boys on Monday night. He's bringing Claire with him."

"Oh, the famous Claire."

"Yes. The bush pilot. I thought maybe we three women should go out and have a drink while the men play hockey."

"You don't think Claire will want to watch Max on the ice?"

"Please. She lives in Alaska. I'm sure she's dying to get away from snow and ice."

"Be great to meet her." Cassie had found Max's combination of brains, wealth and Latin charm to be slightly intimidating. She couldn't imagine him with a bush pilot.

"I only met her once, but I think you'll like her." Serena chuckled softly. "She's quite a character."

"I could definitely use a night out."

"Excellent. We're on, then."

"What if Claire says no?"

"Then we kidnap her."

"No wonder you're a business leader. You always have such sound plans."

Serena pulled out her phone and punched in something. Probably she was already updating her calendar for Monday. Or texting Claire.

"Well, I'd better get back and start on the bedroom. Drop by sometime and check out the progress."

"Love to. Oh, wait, I almost forgot. I have something else for you." And Serena ran to her car, her long legs looking good in tight jeans. Cassie reminded herself that she really needed to fit in more time at the gym.

Serena returned a minute later with a mischievous look on her face and a brown paper bag holding an object about the shape and size of a—*Oh, my gosh, she didn't. Yes, she did*—calendar.

The firefighters' charity calendar. Hunter's finest firefighters, buff and ready to rock your world one month at a time.

She laughed as she opened it slowly, beginning with Mr. January, who was a fine-looking African-American guy with the most amazing pecs she'd ever seen and—

"Oh, don't even think about poring over every month," Serena said. "Flip to June."

Cassie didn't need to be told a second time; her fingers itched to fly past the first five months of the year. Flip, flip, and there he was.

Dylan.

Dylan, shirtless, his firefighting pants slung low on his hips, posing with an ax over his shoulders and a look in his eyes that made her feel as though she were in danger of being scorched. *Oh, my.* Those eyes, those abs, the shoulders.

"I see he has a tattoo," she said finally, feeling a little weak. It was a linked-chain-type thing in dark ink that circled his right bicep. She wondered what it would feel like to put her hand around that tattoo. How far around his muscular arm would her hand even reach? Her palm grew warm thinking about wrapping around that hot skin.

"Let's just say that in my apartment? It's always June."

They snorted with laughter. "Does Adam know?"

"He says when we get married, I have to leave the calendar behind." She glanced at Cassie over the glossy photograph of a grinning Dylan. "He says, 'It's Dylan or me. Make your choice.'"

The color photograph flashed in the sunshine, making Dylan gleam like a bronzed god. "That's got to be a tough choice."

"I tell you, Adam's a great-looking guy. Don't get me wrong. And I will love him to the end of time." She leaned closer. "But a girl can still look."

"Uh-huh." And Cassie wondered how long she could keep looking and remembering to breathe at the same time.

Serena's phone signaled an incoming text. She glanced at it. Frowned. "Speak of the devil."

"Dylan texted you?"

"No. Adam." She put the phone away with a crease between her brows.

Cassie wanted to ask if everything was okay, but before she could say a word, Serena was backing away and waving. "Let me know how it looks when it's up. The chandelier, I mean." And then she was gone.

As she drove home Cassie had to face that her outing, while successful on many fronts, hadn't exactly been the mental cold shower she'd hoped.

Thanks to Mr. June, she felt hotter than when she'd left.

When she pulled into her driveway beside the dusty truck, she immediately grabbed the calendar and stuffed it back in the brown paper bag. She hid it in the chandelier box so her handyman hottie wouldn't see her toting pictures of his hot, half-naked self. Then, leaving the back of her car open, she walked into the house.

"Hi, Dylan, I'm back."

"Okay, I'll come help unload."

"Thanks."

He walked out of the bathroom in one of his threadbare old T-shirts and plaster-dusted jeans. The T-shirt wasn't even tight, but as he moved she felt as if she was seeing him, gorgeous and shirtless once more. Now she knew he had a tat on his upper right bicep, she felt a strange urge to see it in the flesh.

"You okay with that box?" He paused in front of her and she realized she was standing there like a fool. Staring at him.

"Yes. I was only thinking you probably need some water since you've been working in all that dust."

"I was wearing a mask. But yeah, I'll get some. Good idea."

He glanced at the box in her arms. "I'm guessing that's not floor tiles."

She shook her head. "It's a chandelier. For the bedroom. Serena bought it for me as a housewarming gift."

"Awesome. That will look great upstairs." Then he narrowed his gaze. "And why do I have a feeling that my housewarming gift will involve putting it up for you?"

She chuckled. "Because you are so very smart and intuitive."

He shook his head at her as he walked by and she

turned to watch his all-too-amazing back view as he disappeared through the door.

She took the box upstairs, and then pulled out the bag containing the calendar. She felt so foolish having the firefighter calendar at all, and now it was in her bedroom. There wasn't anywhere to hide it. Everything was still in boxes except her chest of drawers. She opened her T-shirt drawer and shoved the calendar in there. Then ran back downstairs.

He was bringing in tile boxes three in a stack, which caused his arm muscles to delineate so she had to drag her gaze away.

She managed two boxes in a stack, but she wasn't striding along as if they were a couple of feathers.

She followed his lead, stacking the boxes in the front hall beside the stairs. There was the kitchen tile, tile for both bathrooms, wall tile, shower tile, tile for the shower floors. She'd had no idea there was so much involved in remodeling a small house. She didn't have the kitchen backsplash yet because she wanted to get her counters first. But she had some ideas, and new magazines seemed to get published every week with new layouts and even newer products.

It was getting so bad that she was beginning to dream of tile and appliances. And maybe a certain guy who was good with an ax.

"Okay, here's the deal," Dylan said, standing with his hands on his hips and looking around Cassie's bedroom with a practiced eye. "If you want the chandelier put up, then I'm going to paint that ceiling first. And if we're painting the ceiling, we might as well get the walls done at the same time."

She looked early-summer ripe in snug denim cutoffs

and a sleeveless blue shirt, her curly hair dancing when she nodded. "Makes sense."

"I'll tackle the ceiling while you do the walls."

She nodded but didn't look exceptionally confident. She'd finished scraping the walls and he could see the places where she'd filled holes. Her pretty hazel eyes seemed as big as the kitten's when she gazed at him. There was a sprinkle of freckles across her nose that he hadn't noticed before.

He might as well know the worst. "What's the last thing you painted?"

"I helped my dad paint my bedroom when I was—" She stopped to think. "Twelve? Thirteen?"

He wondered if he'd gone too long without a woman from the strong way he reacted when she gave him that look. The half-humorous one, as though she were laughing at herself and inviting him to share in her amusement. He had no idea why he found that so sexy, but he couldn't keep the grin off his face. "So you're an experienced bedroom painter, then."

"I might need a refresher course in the finer details."

At least she was keen to get involved, which he liked to see. "Okay, put on some clothes you don't mind getting paint all over and we'll have a lesson in painting 101."

"Okay."

"Great."

He cranked open the stepladder he'd brought upstairs with him. She was hovering in front of her dresser. He prepared to climb the ladder. "Aren't you changing into your grubbies?"

"Uh, I was waiting for you to leave the room."

She hadn't seemed that shy. He felt as though he'd

blundered into one of those female areas that always confused him. "Can't you change in the bathroom?"

"I—um, my—" She glanced at the dresser, looking embarrassed, then back to him. "Could you give me five minutes?"

And suddenly he got it. She probably kept her sex toys in her dresser along with her clothes. Didn't want him getting an eyeful. He hopped off the ladder, trying really hard not to imagine what kind of toys were in that secret drawer. And trying even harder not to picture the two of them playing with them on that big comfy bed underneath the chandelier he was about to install.

6

HE RAN DOWN the stairs and grabbed some paint cloths and plastic sheeting, a roll of painter's tape and rollers, brushes and both the ceiling paint and the wall color. He took the time to give both cans of paint a good stir. When he'd allowed ten minutes to pass, he gathered the painting supplies into a box and pounded back up the stairs, giving her plenty of warning that he was on his way.

Still, he knocked before he walked into Cassie's bedroom. She was fully dressed in jeans that weren't even close to grubby and a long-sleeved T-shirt advertising fish food. She was already unscrewing the old beige plastic switch plate covers from the walls. Excellent. She didn't turn around when he came in, just kept working.

He climbed back up his ladder and tackled taking down the cheap old fixture that had probably been hanging up here for the entire life of the house. Who looked at something that ugly every night for fifty years? Right before they went to sleep?

Which sent his mind skidding back to those images again. The atmosphere in the room was different.

Charged. Heating up. He suspected it was him thinking about what secrets were hidden in her sex-toy drawer. He told himself to stop. He was working for her, not sleeping with her. But like the proverbial elephant, the more he tried to stop wondering what was in her secret stash, the more his imagination conjured up every toy he'd ever seen, heard of or dreamed up.

He took down the light fixture—dead flies, old cobwebs and all—and carried it downstairs in a large box to add to his growing trash pile.

Back in the bedroom, he found Cassie was unscrewing the last of the outlet covers. A neat pile of them sat in a corner, all the screws gathered together. He liked the orderly way she worked.

"Okay," he said, "when you're done with those, we'll cover everything up and then I'll paint the ceiling while you…?"

Together, they pulled her bed away from the wall. He didn't have to tell her how to lift, he noted. She bent from the knees and lifted like a pro. They moved her dresser away from the wall and not for one second did he allow himself to think about what was inside that dresser. Nope. There definitely wasn't a pink vibrator in there. *Stop it.* No fur-lined handcuffs. He wasn't even thinking about the possibility. No blindfolds or massage oils. He was relieved when they finally had the room cleared of boxes and the bit of remaining furniture away from the walls. He left Cassie draping plastic over her bed while he prepped the ceiling for painting.

Since he was painting the ceiling the same white as before, he contented himself with giving it a good rub with a dry cloth, removing old cobwebs and any loose dirt or dust that might adhere to the wet paint. He moved the ladder around, doing a quadrant at a time.

He got Cassie washing the walls down so the paint job would look professional. He could hear the soft splash when she dipped her sponge into the water and the swishing sound as she washed the walls.

He worked fast, wanting to get to the painting. Not that he loved painting ceilings—it always gave him a crick in his neck—but he held on to the image of the completed room and that helped him get through the tedious parts.

She hadn't put on music and he didn't want to impose his choices on her, so they worked in silence. He said, "How's it going down there?"

"I'm sick at how dirty this water is."

"This whole room's going to be clean and fresh by the time you go to bed tonight."

"Good."

"You might want to sleep in the other bedroom tonight, though. It will smell like paint in here." What was the matter with him? Could he mention her and beds in the same sentence a few more times?

"Good idea," she said. "I'll get the guest room made up."

"I saw a bunch of diving stuff in your garage. You're a diver?"

"I am. I've been diving since I was a kid. I grew up in Southern California, so the water was a lot warmer. I spent every second I could in the water. Surfing, diving, swimming. Still do." He heard the slosh as she dunked her sponge and squeezed it out. "Though up here I'm in a wet suit most of the year. How about you? Do you dive?"

"I've tried it. But I'm more of an aboveground kind of guy. I play hockey, basketball, stuff like that."

He imagined living in eternal sunshine. "Do you miss it? California?"

He heard the sponge stop moving, as though she were contemplating the question. "I do sometimes. I miss the weather and my family. I moved up here for the job, but once I got used to all the rain, I really came to appreciate the green. The forests and mountains. I still go back a few times a year, but this is home for me now. Especially now that I've bought a house."

"A house is only as permanent as you make it. I buy and sell houses all the time. Fix them up and move on."

"Why do I get the impression you don't like feeling trapped?" she said. He could hear the smile in her voice.

He thought about that. How could a woman who barely even knew him throw out a comment like that? Was he giving off some kind of vibe? So he asked her. "What makes you say that?"

Once more the sponge stopped moving. "I don't know. I get the sense that you like to keep things loose. And Serena told me you won some kind of eternal-bachelor contest with your friends."

"Not eternal," he corrected her. "Last Bachelor Standing. I'll get married." Though even saying the word caused a constriction in his throat. "Someday."

"So I was wrong?"

Was she? Now his rag stopped moving as he took a moment to think about whether or not he felt easily trapped. "I don't know. I don't spend a lot of time contemplating the lint in my navel. I've been in the same job for ten years." Though he might not have it for much longer if he wasn't careful. "I've got the same friends I've had since I was a kid. That's commitment. Right?"

"Absolutely." But she didn't sound completely convinced. Sure, most of the guys he knew who were his age and even younger were married. Some had kids, and he always imagined he'd do it, too. The time had never been right. The woman had never been right. Or maybe he'd never been ready.

"People change," he said. "Adam and Max were as bad as me six months ago. Now they're both headed for the wedding chapel."

"You don't sound envious."

"I think Serena's a great gal. And Claire seems like she suits Max. But no, I'm not envious. Except that I figure they'll both have a lot less time to spend playing hockey and hanging out with the guys once they're hitched and start having kids."

"You'll have to find some younger guys to hang out with."

She said it perfectly seriously, but he got the idea that she might be suggesting he was immature. Which was probably true.

"How about you? Do you feel like buying a house is permanent?"

"I think I do. Even though I understand that people change houses on average every five to ten years, my folks are still in the same house they bought when they got married. I bought a place I could grow into."

"You planning to fill it with a husband and babies?" He didn't mean to sound sarcastic but he thought it might have slipped out.

"Sure. I hope I meet the right guy. But if I don't, I've got a good career, and I'll have a nice home as soon as you finish renovating it for me."

It was weird that it sounded a little lonely when she described what was essentially his own existence: a house he was fixing up, a great career and no plans to outfit a nursery any time soon.

He climbed down off the ladder, picking it up to move it to the next quadrant of the ceiling. He heard the swish of the bucket, not registering that the swishing sound was much closer than before until he collided with a warm back. Dylan always moved fast. He was one hundred and eighty-five pounds of impatient, so when he struck an object it tended to fly.

Cassie was no exception. With a startled cry, she tumbled. He grabbed her, all his training and instincts kicking in before conscious thought, and he tossed her to the bed, his own momentum carrying him in the same direction.

They fell to the bed. She somehow ended up underneath him, the sponge still in her up-flung hand so a fan of water sprayed out onto the plastic-covered canvas drop sheet.

He glanced down into her face, surprise and shock registering. Then he noticed that she was warm and soft beneath him on the bed and all the attraction he'd been pretending he didn't feel roared to the surface. He didn't even think, because if he thought before he acted he wouldn't do half the things in his life that he did.

He leaned down. Not too fast, not wanting to take his mouth where it wasn't wanted. But he'd felt the answering attraction and he felt it now. She didn't roll away or push him off. She opened her lips in a kind of breathless sigh. When he kissed her he felt the moment their lips touched that it had been inevitable from the second he'd walked into her house.

She was gorgeous, sweet, single, and they were together a lot in a small house. He kissed her, going deeper than he'd intended until she moaned deep in her throat. When she started to move against him, he felt his arousal shoot up.

He pushed a hand into her hair, changed the angle so he could kiss her more deeply. She reached for his arms. Not to stop him, but to run her hands up his forearms, over his elbows and up to his biceps. Then she did a funny thing. She wrapped her hands around the thickest part of the muscle and squeezed as though she were putting a blood pressure cuff on him.

She muttered something he couldn't understand. Then those wet hands kept moving, leaving damp patches where she touched him through the T-shirt.

He wanted so much and he wanted it all now, but dimly an alarm began to ring as his thinking brain finally caught up to his prehistoric brain. What the hell was he doing? He was supposed to be fixing up this woman's house, not jumping her luscious bones.

He pulled away slowly, feeling stunned. He stared down at her, finding her lips wet and swollen from his kisses. Her eyes were unfocused, but as he stared down at her, he saw the awareness flood back.

He felt turned on, awkward and clumsy all at once. "We should, uh,—"

"Get back to work," she finished for him, her voice a little husky.

"Yeah." He rolled off her. Decided there was no way he could continue working in this room with her in the same small space and that kiss between them. He stood up. "I'm finished prepping the ceiling. I'll get the roller extension and give the paint another stir." And find a few other things to keep him busy until she was clear.

She scrambled to her feet right after him, pulling down her T-shirt self-consciously. "I should finish the walls."

"Great. Give me a shout when you're done."

"I will."

They didn't look at each other. He wondered what she was thinking. Wondered what he was thinking. Decided he didn't want to know.

He headed out of the room with his stepladder and a raging case of unrelieved lust.

7

"I'VE NEVER FELT more foolish in my life," Cassie said over her second glass of merlot at the wine bar the three women had adjourned to on Monday night while the three guys took to the ice to practice for Badges on Ice.

Claire hadn't needed to be kidnapped. She'd been delighted to hang out with the other women while her fiancé played hockey with the boys.

Cassie liked her right away. She was down-to-earth, funny and pretty rather than beautiful. She didn't look anything like the kind of trophy bride Cassie assumed billionaires always mated with. The ring on her finger was surprisingly tasteful. The solitaire was certainly sizable and no doubt the diamond was flawless, but it suited the hand of a woman who flew planes in Alaska for a living.

By the end of the first glass of wine the three women were well on the way to becoming fast friends.

Cassie had had no one to talk to since the kiss had happened on Saturday, and to her surprise, she felt comfortable discussing it with Serena and Claire. It wasn't as if she had much else to talk about. She seemed to be obsessed with a very short tumble on the bed that had consisted of nothing but some deep, heavy kissing. She couldn't believe she was making such a big deal of it.

"I think a lot of women would use another word than *foolish* to describe rolling around on the bed with Dylan," Serena said.

"See, that's the thing. Do I want to be one of the many women Dylan's rolled around on the bed with?"

"Has it happened again?" Claire asked.

"No!" That was the worst part. Not only had she and Dylan never referred to the steamy scene again, but he'd gone out of his way to make sure he was working far away from her whenever they were both in the house. "Does he think I'm dogmeat?" she finally exploded.

Serena bit back a smile. "I doubt he thinks you're dogmeat. Maybe he felt it was inappropriate to make a move on a woman he's working for."

"It was. Wildly inappropriate. But it was one of those crazy moments that just happen."

"Indulge me," Serena said. "Describe your close encounter with Mr. June for me one more time."

"Stop it!" Cassie said, laughing in spite of herself.

"You have to admit, it sounds like something out of one of those meet-cute movies."

"Except that this is my life and the man is in my house every day. Not acting like he's smitten by me. Acting like he deeply regrets kissing me."

"What are you going to do?" Claire asked.

"Keep drinking." She raised her glass.

"No. Really."

"I guess I'll continue to pretend it didn't happen. Maybe spend more time at work so I don't see him so much."

"You can't let the man keep you out of your own home. That's ridiculous."

"You could talk to him," Claire suggested.

She popped a peanut in her mouth. "What would I say?"

"I don't know, but maybe a frank discussion would clear the air."

"Serena?" The woman was a professional business coach. Shouldn't she have some ideas? Somehow, Cassie felt that her good friend wasn't taking her embarrassing intimacy with Mr. June as seriously as she should.

"It's a good idea," she said after a moment. "You could tell him that you want to clear the air and you don't blame him for what happened."

She stared at her friend. "Is that what you think he's feeling? That I blame him?"

Serena shrugged her elegant shoulders. "Who knows what he's thinking or feeling? That's why Claire has a good point. You won't make things worse if you bring it up."

Oh, what she wouldn't give to go back to the Time Before the Kiss when she and Dylan were easy around each other. She'd made him coffee in the morning; he'd carried the kitten around on his shoulder and made her fixer-upper a little closer to a real home each day.

"Here, here, here," Max bellowed as Dylan hooked the puck away from a winger who couldn't seem to skate and pass at the same time.

He heard his buddy and, understanding he was signaling that he was open, took a quick glance in the direction of the voice, set up his shot and passed the puck to Max.

While this was going on, Dylan was speeding toward the opposing net. They'd practiced this a million times as a drill; it was always so sweet when it worked in a game.

Max sent the puck sailing toward Dylan, who slammed that baby so hard the goalie was on his ass before he realized the puck had sunk home.

The rush of adrenaline that always soared when a play went down so perfectly spiked through Dylan's blood. The three guys surged together, along with the rest of their team and celebrated the goal with manly hugs and backslaps.

He loved this game. He felt the cold air on his face as he took his position for a face-off, knowing he was exactly where he was supposed to be. There were so few times in his life that he felt that, especially these days, with his suspension keeping him from his job and that stupid kiss keeping him from the ease he'd formerly enjoyed with his sexy client.

As the game progressed, he gloried in the feel of his skates carving into cold, clean ice, his muscles working hard as he sped around the rink, at moments feeling as though he was flying. He fell into the zone, where all that mattered was figuring out where the puck was, where his key teammates were, how to get around the opposition. They were so ready to take Badges on Ice this year. So very ready.

And because he was in the zone he was rewarded with one of those magical moments when he was in the right place at the perfect moment to catch a breakaway. He scooped up the puck with the same ease and familiarity with which he scooped up the kitten he carried around with him so much of the day. He protected the puck from anybody who thought they might like to take it off him and turned on the jets.

He glanced around to see if he had a passing oppor-

tunity and what he saw instead was a scoring opportunity. The goalie came out, eyes gleaming behind his
helmet, trying to guess Dylan's next move. In his pe-
ripheral vision he saw the defenders race to catch him.
He faked right, and in a move that was all about fast-
twitch-muscle control, one of the things he worked on
every day at the gym, shot the puck left.

Goalie almost got to it.

Almost.

His goal won them the game.

The usual backslapping and manly hugging ensued.
There were never tons of spectators at their games, but
he did a victory pose anyway for their small cheering
section—mostly the benched guys, the coach and a few
wives, girlfriends and work buddies. For a moment he
wished Cassie were there, giving him her big smile.
Then he shook the thought off.

He was getting soft.

"How's THE RENO project going?" Max asked as the three
men relaxed in the dressing room, their usual cold postgame beers in hand.

"Fine."

"You don't sound very happy. Usually you love home
renos."

Dylan scowled down at his beer. "I screwed up,
okay?"

"What did you do?" Adam suddenly leaned forward,
all attention. Dylan knew his cop buddy felt responsible that he'd told Cassie to hire him, so he hastened
to reassure him. "It's nothing to do with my work. I'm
doing a great job."

"Then what?"

"I kissed her."

There was silence from both his sandbox buddies. Finally he glanced up. "Well?"

Max and Adam exchanged glances. They both had the red cheeks and sweaty hair of men who'd skated hard for the better part of two hours. Max spoke. "I was waiting for the rest."

"That's it. There is no rest." He put his beer down on the bench. Picked it up again. Took a pull. "I was prepping her bedroom ceiling, she was washing walls. It was nothing. Then I don't know what happened. I wasn't paying attention. I got down from the ladder and moved one way and she must have picked up her bucket to move to a new section of wall, and we collided and ended up falling on the bed. Together."

"And you kissed her," Adam prompted.

"Yeah."

"Then what?" Max asked.

"Then nothing. I'm not going to hit on a woman I'm working for. It's crazy."

"Crazy doesn't usually stop you," Max commented.

"Well, this time it does."

"So you kissed her and then what?"

"Did what any sensible man would do. I pretended it never happened."

Adam and Max shared another glance. Both nodded. Being sensible men.

"So there's no problem, then."

This was why he'd brought the kiss up in the first place. "It's kind of weird, you know?"

"Has she said anything?"

"No. But we're different with each other now. I feel like I need to keep my distance and she is acting the same way."

"I wouldn't worry about it. Get on with your work and you'll both put it behind you and move on."

"You really think so?"

"That or you'll get so horny you both throw off all your clothes and go at it like rabbits. Hard to tell which way this will roll."

He studied the tiled floor of the changeroom. "Maybe I should date."

"Date? Who?"

"I don't know. Maybe I'm acting like a guy who isn't getting any because I'm a guy who isn't getting any."

Adam sniffed. Wiped sweat. "Not that I'm an expert on relationships, but I don't think it's going to be a great idea to start dating other women when you've kissed Cassie. She might get the wrong impression."

Max nodded. "She might think you're a slut."

They all snorted with laughter and then Adam said, "I need you guys to go get measured for tuxes. For the wedding."

"I already own one," Max reminded them.

"A tux? Really?" Dylan complained even though he'd been prepared to force himself into clothing that felt more confining than his bunker gear.

"You're my two best men. You have to look good. My wife-to-be expects it."

Dylan thought that having two best men was a bunch of new-age crap, but then he wondered how he would feel if Adam had chosen Max instead of him, how any of the three could choose one man over the other as his closest friend, and knew it was impossible. One day he'd end up with two best men, too. Unless he did the sensible thing and eloped.

Or stayed single.

They finished their beers, then showered and packed their bags. "Well," Adam said, "shall we join the girls?"

Max nodded and the two started out of the change-room.

"What do you mean, join the girls?" Dylan demanded. Since he wasn't an engaged man nobody ever told him anything.

They turned in unison. "Claire and Serena and Cassie are at a wine bar. We told the girls we'd stop by," Adam said, his keys jingling in his hand as though he was in a big hurry to get going.

"I don't know." He felt weird about seeing Cassie in a social context. Well, he felt weird seeing her in any context since his stupidity.

"Aw, come on. The sooner you start acting normal around her, the easier it will be."

He should go home. He should catch up on TV. Pay some bills.

Then he thought about Cassie being stuck alone at a table with two sets of wedding-planning lovebirds and knew he couldn't do it to her. "Okay. One quick drink and I'm out of there."

They met up at an upscale wine bar Dylan had never been in. He was more of a beer-and-nachos kind of guy.

The three met up in the parking lot and walked in together. He saw Cassie right away. He'd never seen her dressed up to go out before and he couldn't help but notice that she cleaned up real nice. She wore a green top that showed off bare arms and a touch of cleavage. She wore bright lipstick that showed off her kissable lips and her white teeth, which were currently on display as she laughed at something one of the other women was saying.

That was one of the things he liked about her, he realized. She laughed a lot. Didn't seem as though she took life too seriously. You got to know a lot about a person when you were renovating their house. It was a stressful, dirty process, especially when the homeowner was living on site. It brought out the worst in most people. Kitchens got torn out, plumbing got moved, dust and noise were everywhere. Yet Cassie seemed to take it all in stride. She remained good-humored when the tile box he opened was the wrong color and when the fridge she'd chosen was out of stock until the next millennium.

She was willing to pitch in and if she didn't know how to do something, she was willing to learn.

As he walked forward he realized, to his shock, that in the two days they'd been apart he'd actually missed her. He'd missed the easy way they'd joked around each other and she'd shared her ideas, asked his opinion. He'd asked her to make choices, offered suggestions. They'd had an easy give-and-take. He realized he wanted that back.

So when she turned her head and caught him looking at her, he didn't immediately glance away. He sent her an easy smile. After a second, she returned it.

The three men walked up. Adam kissed Serena and said, "Welcome to Washington," to Claire and kissed her on the cheek. Then, of course, Cassie got the cheek-kissing treatment. Max, being South American, with testosterone in his veins where blood should be, grabbed the opportunity to kiss three hot women.

What was Dylan supposed to do?

He kissed Serena on the cheek. Kissed Claire on the cheek. Turned to Cassie. Knew he'd look like a huge idiot if he didn't kiss her, too. He reached in, noticed her scent right away—he smelled it at odd times around the house—a faint floral scent with a hint of spice. Her skin was so smooth and being this close to her reminded him all over again of how she'd felt beneath him, hot and sweet. How her lips had felt under his, how she'd tasted. How her hair felt in his hands. Her ripe, squirming body.

Shit.

Since the other guys had grabbed seats beside their wives-to-be, he took a seat beside Cassie at the table. "How's it going?"

"Good."

He hadn't seen her since Friday. He'd left today before she'd returned home.

"The bathroom tile looks great," she said. It had been the job he'd started this morning. The plumber had moved everything, so today they'd put in the flooring and then he'd started the tile.

"You made a good choice." Then, because it had surprised him, he said, "You bought cat food."

If the change of subject surprised her, tile to cat food, she didn't let on.

"I ran out of tuna." She bit her lip when he merely raised an eyebrow. "I need to fatten her up a bit before sending her to the shelter. She's so skinny. People might not realize she's healthy."

"Or, you could adopt her."

"Cats can live twenty years," she said in a tone that suggested she'd been thinking about it.

"I think you'll outlast her."

She choked on a giggle. "You know what I mean."

"Commitment. Yeah."

He knew that a cat had not been part of her plan when she bought a house, but he'd also seen her at her computer, the kitten a snoozing ball in her lap. His money was on the cat.

"So, how are the wedding plans coming?" Adam asked Claire.

Dylan's attention jerked toward his teammate.

Seriously? These guys liked to smash other men into the boards during intense hockey games. They chased criminals and ran multimillion-dollar companies. Were they really going to talk about wedding planning like those people on reality TV shows?

"I've barely started," Claire said. "There's not much to choose from in Spruce Bay, Alaska. Luckily we have the internet. But I am shopping for my dress and all my accessories while I'm here."

"I've got a list of the best places," Serena promised. "Maybe we can go together?"

"Oh, I'd love that." She turned to Cassie. "You should come, too. It would be more fun with three."

"Sure. Why not?"

Dylan started to feel the way he knew his tux would feel for Adam's wedding. As if the collar was too tight and he was slowly choking.

Luckily the wine bar condescended to serve beer. And the gourmet burger wasn't bad.

Once they got off wedding talk, the evening was surprisingly fun. He felt the muscle exhaustion from a good workout, the company of good people, and there was a lot of laughter and joking around as they settled in and relaxed.

After they'd finished, Serena said, "I hate to break up the party, but I've got an early meeting." She was giving a coaching presentation in Seattle and also had a book signing planned.

Adam and Max had driven in together in Max's car, so Adam said, "I'll come with you."

"Do you mind dropping me off?" Cassie asked.

"Of course." Then he realized the girls had also driven in together.

Even before Adam shot him the glance of a man who was going to be deprived of his sexy fiancée for a whole day and couldn't waste a single minute, he was already saying, "I can drive you home, Cassie. It's on my way."

"Oh." He got the sudden feeling she wished she'd brought her own ride. "Well, if you're sure."

The three couples all drifted to their cars and shouted out good-nights.

He opened the passenger door for Cassie because it made him feel like a jerk not to. She flashed him a smile and had to step up into the truck, which made her black skirt rise, giving him a nice glimpse of thigh.

He saw her settled, then banged the truck door shut and rounded to his own side. *Be cool,* he said to himself. *Don't mention the kiss and everything will go back to normal.*

8

BE A GROWN-UP, Cassie said to herself as she waited for Dylan to get into the truck. This was the perfect opportunity to talk to him about that kiss. To clear the air. They'd get through a couple of awkward minutes and then they could return to the easy work relationship they'd shared.

He started up the truck, backed out of the space and as he headed forward said, "You know what I was thinking?"

Oh, good, she thought. He was going to bring up the kiss. "What were you thinking?"

"That we should move the dishwasher."

"Move the dishwasher?" That's what he wanted to talk about? They'd all but had a date tonight, had been strained with each other since that crazy kiss, and he wanted to talk about moving a dishwasher?

But, of course, the house reno was her baby. Right now the location of her dishwasher actually was more vital than the meaning of one kiss. If he'd planned to derail her—and he probably had—he couldn't have picked a better topic. "Where do you want to move it?"

In the dim light she caught the flash of his teeth.

"Not out of the kitchen or anything. I was thinking that if we situated it on the left of the sink instead of the right then it ends up closer to the cupboards and the cutlery drawer. Might be more efficient."

She pulled up the kitchen design as though she'd loaded a CAD program into her brain. Nodded enthusiastically then, realizing he had his eyes on the road, said, "Yes. I think that's a really good idea."

"You know, you're an easy person to work for. You're open to new ideas. You'd be surprised how many people want to put everything back exactly the way it was. Drives me nuts."

"Sometimes change is good."

There was silence for a few moments. He fiddled with the music. Found an oldies station that was playing Marvin Gaye. Did Dylan even notice that Marvin was crooning about sexual feelings?

"I think I found some cork flooring I like."

He nodded. As though he'd expected she'd take that suggestion, as well. Well, he might be a little full of himself but damn, he was good.

Various flooring surfaces kept them occupied until he pulled into her drive. She turned to thank him for driving her home and found him looking at her mouth. She didn't think he'd intended it, more that his gaze had strayed there and got stuck.

Oh, the heck with it. If two intelligent women like Claire and Serena thought she should bring up the other night, then she figured she'd better take their advice just as she took Dylan's advice on renos. Heaven knew both women were more successful with relationships than she was.

"Dylan."

"Mmm?"

"About that kiss the other day…"

His gaze jerked up to hers. "That was a mistake," he said quickly.

She felt stung. All she'd wanted to do was clear the air. "It was?" she said before she could prevent the words from escaping.

"No." He shook his head as though he found the whole thing as confusing as she did. "It was great. I mean, you're amazing. It's just that—"

"You're working for me."

"Exactly." He flicked off his seat belt. Moved a little closer.

If this wasn't the most ridiculous conversation she'd ever had. She unclicked her own seat belt. "Me kissing you could be construed as sexual harassment in the workplace."

"Just what I was thinking," he agreed, his big, burn-scarred hand moving to cup the back of her head.

"How do we handle that?"

"Probably best if I kiss you."

"I think that's a good—" She never finished the sentence. His mouth closed over the word *idea,* taking that and any other idea she might have had right out of her head. She leaned into his warmth, unable to prevent the longing she'd felt ever since they'd first touched. He was so warm, so solid, so damned sexy. She felt the strength of his muscles, and when he took over her mouth she felt the dash of recklessness that would prevent this man from ever being called dull.

At least this time she wasn't splashed with dirty water from washing walls. Her hair was styled; she wore makeup and her going-out clothes. He smelled of clean male and whatever he'd used for his postgame shower. Some kind of shower gel that smelled like eucalyptus. And underneath that she smelled him. His skin, his hot, sexy self.

She sighed as she gave in to sensation. As discussions went they hadn't exactly had one, but at the moment she really didn't care. He was kissing her and she realized how much she wanted to be kissed by this capable, exciting man.

He touched her in all the right places, treating her body with delicacy, not grabbing and groping. Oh, this man knew his way around a woman's body and she suddenly knew that she wanted him to have all of it. And soon.

He pulled slowly back, breathing a little heavily. "Well."

She tried to push her hair back into place but it was hopeless. She licked her already wet lips. "Would you like to see the new duvet cover I bought for the bedroom? It looks so good with the wall color and the chandelier you put up for me."

He eased back a little, his eyes glinting. "That wouldn't be more sexual harassment, would it, boss?"

"Do you want it to be?" Her words sounded heavy, almost as heavy as the feelings pooling in her belly.

"Yes, ma'am."

"Come on, then." She pushed open her door and jumped down. He turned off the truck engine and followed her. She almost fumbled the key in the lock, she was so full of anticipation—and maybe a touch of nervousness. What if it was awful? What if he—or she—was disappointed? Then they'd have to work together and it could be even more awkward. What if he thought this was a hookup?

What if he didn't?

Oh, no wonder she was no good at relationships, she

chided herself as she started up the stairs, feeling him behind her, as hot as her fantasies. If she started worrying about consequences before she'd even done anything, they'd both end up disappointed.

Then they reached the top of the stairs and he pulled her back against him, kissing the back of her neck so she shivered.

Consequences?

Disappointment?

Not an option.

She flipped on the chandelier as she entered, taking a moment even through the haze of lust to enjoy the new space. The chandelier sparkled like something out of a fairy tale, casting soft light on the blue-and-yellow duvet cover. The soft blue walls were perfect. She'd bought cushions in blue and yellow and then thrown caution to the wind and added a couple in French-country fabrics. They didn't match the bedspread but they pulled the room together, as an HGTV decorator would say.

The side tables were mismatched pieces she'd bought at a Goodwill store years ago and painted white. Shabby chic. She still liked them. She was waiting on artwork and the headboard until she found the perfect pieces. She wasn't in a rush; she'd have this house for a long, long time.

"It looks fantastic," he said, duly admiring the room. "I'll get onto your en suite as soon as we finish the main bathroom and the kitchen."

She nodded. Then realized that as much as she loved her new chandelier, she did not want to make love under its somewhat merciless gaze. Crossing to the bedside table, she flicked on one of the crystal lamps that had belonged to her grandmother.

He didn't comment, merely flipped off the overhead

switch so the room immediately became more dimly lit. For a second she was sorry, realizing that if he couldn't see her completely clearly, the same would be true for her—and she really wanted to see him in all his glorious detail.

She was about to have Mr. June in her bed.

For a moment she felt the grip of uncertainty. What had she done? Or, more correctly, what was she contemplating doing? If one kiss had made her and her contractor handyman strained around each other, what would full intimacy do?

As she turned to him, wondering if she should call the evening off, she found him already in front of her. The man moved like the cat.

He pulled her against him so she bumped chest to chest, feeling his strength once more. All it took was one touch and her worries disappeared. He had enough sureness for both of them.

He tipped back her head, taking full advantage of her mouth, kissing her as though all he'd ever wanted in the entirety of his life was to kiss her. She was moving from zero to supersonic way too fast. She felt the surge of lust take her and toss her as he moved his mouth on hers, teasing her with his tongue. She could taste beer and hot, healthy male. As he pushed his body against hers, she amended that to hot, healthy, thoroughly aroused male.

She threw her arms around him and began to rub her hands down his back, enjoying the feel of his strong muscles enticing her beneath his shirt.

Before she could plunge her hands beneath the cotton to the hot skin, he eased her silky top over her head, so she had to release him long enough to get her hands up. Her skin was so sensitive she felt the slide of fabric like a caress.

Even though she wanted to put her hands under his shirt so badly they tingled, he held her away from him, his gaze devouring her breasts in the going-out underwear she was so glad she'd worn. She'd have to remember to thank Serena for that last trip they'd taken to Victoria's Secret, when her friend had pretty much forced her to buy lacy nonsense even though she didn't have anyone to wear it for.

"And what are you going to do when you have someone to wear it for and you didn't buy it?" Serena had argued. "I'm telling you not as your friend, but as a very successful performance coach. If you wear sexy underwear you are fifty-eight percent more likely to have great sex with an amazing man." Cassie had glanced at the department-store generic beige bra hunched on the change room's only chair. "You wear that and you won't want to get undressed, never mind have sex."

But Cassie wasn't born yesterday. She'd crossed her arms over the admittedly delicious black lacy cups she was trying on. "Fifty-eight percent? You are making that up."

Serena had remained as serious as a nun at confession. "Fifty-eight point two, to be precise."

"Oh, well, now that you've mentioned the extra point two, I'd better get the matching panties."

At the time she'd been convinced her friend was joking. Now she wasn't so sure. There was something about donning nice lingerie that definitely put a girl in the mood. And to have a man like Dylan staring at her chest as though those lacy bra cups were serving up two dishes of heaven was enough to get her even more revved up.

"You—" he kissed the top of one breast "—are—" he kissed the top of the other "—gorgeous." And he reached around and snapped open the catch.

She moved her shoulders and arms so the bra slipped off.

He pulled her to him wordlessly, crushing her lips with his mouth, his hands going everywhere at once. His greed and impatience fired hers. She dragged at his shirt, his belt, bumped into his hands trying to perform the same tasks.

She almost growled in frustration as she fumbled at his belt until he pushed her hands away and did the job himself, though not very smoothly. He shoved his jeans down his legs, kicking them off with impatience. His briefs followed; his shirt was over his head and sailing into the newly painted walls.

Pulling back the coverlet on the bed, he gently pushed her so she fell into the soft, cool sheets—the new ones she'd bought as part of her bedroom do-over. Maybe her life was following suit, she thought dimly as she felt the cool air on her naked torso. Maybe redecorating her bedroom had given her the remaining 41.8-percent chance of having great sex with an amazing stud.

She liked that idea. That she might transform along with the house into the woman she dreamed of becoming.

As she gazed her fill at that glorious man standing naked beside the bed, he bent and removed her skirt, pulling as she wriggled so she was left in nothing but a lacy black thong.

"You're killing me," he said, his voice a husky whisper.

"Don't die yet. Not until I've had at least three orgasms."

He chuckled, "Greedy, huh?"

"You have no idea."

9

HE FOLLOWED HER down onto the bed, his body so hot against hers. His hands were everywhere, exciting her, learning her. She felt soft and pliable compared to his firefighting-toned body. And yet his mouth was so soft, tender almost, as it traced the line of her collarbone, dipping to her breasts. He licked the underside and she felt like screaming. The sensations were racing too fast for her to keep up. Her nipples ached for his touch, already tingling in anticipation.

And as he put his mouth on one aching point, he reached down, slipping his hand into her panties, sliding to her core, where she was already slick with desire, and playing with her even as his mouth was busy at her nipples.

Orgasm one hit her so fast she barely had time to register how close she was. She arched against his fingers, pushing herself higher. He took her lead, giving her what she needed until her back arched right off the bed and her cries echoed off the walls.

He stroked her softly, bringing her down slowly, kissing her breasts easily until her panting subsided.

She stared up at the ceiling, feeling as if she might

as well have worn a neon sign that said, Chick Who Seriously Needs to Get Laid. It had been so long. She eyed him. "That was—"

His smile cut her off almost before his words did, so delighted did he seem. "Amazing," he said, finishing the sentence in a whole different direction than she would have gone. "That was absolutely amazing."

She threw her arms around him. Kissing him noisily. "Your turn," she said. "Condoms are in the side table."

"Not so fast," he said, rising so he could look down at her probably flushed face. "Can you do that again?"

A warm flood of possibilities filled her. She tilted her head, glanced up through her lashes. "Let's find out."

"Oh, I do like a challenge."

She could feel the rigidity in him, and she knew it wasn't as easy to hold himself back as he wanted her to believe. She tried to tell him that she wanted him inside her as much as she could sense he wanted to be there, but then his mouth began to travel south and she forgot how to form words.

Down her belly his lips traveled, bringing her sex roaring back from satiated to starved. He took his time, though, making her wait. He relieved her of her panties in one smooth move, then kissed his way back up her legs, explored the bumps of her hip bones with his tongue, eased her legs apart with his big hands.

She was still swollen and slick from her recent climax, so she hovered halfway back up that peak. She wanted to hold on forever, to enjoy the delicious feel of his tongue on her, but her body didn't feel like waiting. It seemed much more interested in Blow Me Apart, *Now!*

And so, in short order, he did.

"Damn," he murmured, "you are one responsive

woman." He said it admiringly, gazing at her as though she'd done something particularly amazing.

"I was built that way," she said, refusing to take credit. "But I am grateful all the same."

"And so am I."

She loved that he enjoyed her sexuality as much as she did.

"I want you to come inside me."

"Okay. Don't have to be asked twice." He reached for her night table, and she didn't bother to help him— she enjoyed watching the stretch and twist of muscles. He put a fan of condoms on the table beside them and she didn't comment.

She watched him sheath himself, swiftly and efficiently, and knew she'd take on that job next time in order to get that impressive piece of manhood in her hands. She also suspected that he probably had too much steam built up for her to get involved quite yet. So she watched.

Then, instead of getting on top of her as she'd imagined he would, he hoisted her up to sitting and scooted in behind her, his back against the wall. She really needed to do something about a nice headboard.

When he lifted her hips, she followed his lead, and felt him ease her slowly onto his rigid cock. Oh, it was a good thing her body was so slippery and relaxed with satisfaction, because Mr. June wasn't only big in the pecs and biceps. He was large everywhere.

And as he slowly entered her body she felt stretched in places she didn't think she'd ever been stretched. "Oh," she moaned. "Oh."

"You okay?" He stopped, holding her still.

She turned her head until she could kiss him. "I am more than okay," she whispered.

He nodded and continued easing her down onto him until he was all the way in and she was settled on his lap.

He opened her legs and, reaching around, began to play with her again. "Oh, not fair, I want to—"

"What?" he whispered in her hair, his voice husky. "What do you want?"

"I want to move, I want to—"

"You are moving. You're wriggling and pulsing and so hot I'm going to explode inside you any second now," he promised.

She felt him moving a little inside her, and she felt his fingers stroking her hot button outside her and she felt his chest, hot and huffing out and in with his labored breath at her back, and she felt as though it was too much. Too much stimulation, too much of a good thing, she'd never be able to hold on, she couldn't control her hips and didn't even try—she began to do a seriously out-of-control lap dance. He kept up with her rhythm with his fingers, stroking her until she could feel the pressure rising, the gorgeous pressure, and the beautiful, strong cock pushing up inside her only added to the imminent explosion.

She wanted to tell him, warn him, but it was already too late. She threw back her head so it banged his shoulder, felt the shock waves begin to rise and then she was thrown forward, she was on her hands and knees and he stayed with her, driving into her even as she drove back against him again and again, until she quaked and cried out and her world careened out of control.

She heard the low roar behind her as Dylan joined in.

As they collapsed on the bed, Dylan said, "And that's three."

She turned to him, giving a lazy chuckle. When she

caught her breath enough to talk, she said, "Can you do that?"

His sleepy, sexy blues regarded her. "What, come three times?"

She nodded.

"Not bang, bang, bang, like you." He pulled her over so her head was resting on his chest, where his heart thudded comfortably beneath her ear. "But maybe bang, pause, bang, pause, bang."

"Okay."

"Okay, what?"

"Okay, so this is a pause."

He pulled her closer. "You are so my kind of woman."

10

CASSIE WOKE SUDDENLY, wondering why she was so hot, and then became aware that a very warm male body was pressed up to hers. In that instant of swimming between sleep and consciousness, she felt the memories flood back. They'd never discussed Dylan staying the night—she suspected they'd both passed out at some point. But, she recalled smugly, bang, pause, bang, pause, bang worked just fine for her new lover.

It had worked fine for her, too.

Dawn was letting a gauzy film of light into the room, enough for her to watch him and admire the strong features in his face. When he wasn't joking around and teasing her, Dylan had a serious side to him.

His right arm was flung up over his head in sleep and she was fascinated to see that the chain tattoo on his upper arm sported links of some sort on the underside of his arm.

She was squinting, trying to distinguish the significance when she realized he was awake and watching her. Had his breathing changed? When she looked at him, she found his eyes open and on hers. She felt the smile pull at her lips.

"Hi," she said.

"Hi." He yawned. "What time is it?"

"Early."

She reached out and traced the line of his tattoo. "Tell me about your tat."

"It's a chain."

"I can see that. What are these symbols here?" There were three of them on the underside of his arm, where she imagined they were mostly hidden from view.

He turned his head as though he might have forgotten they were there and was seeing them for the first time. There was a short pause, which she found interesting. Most people were only too happy to talk about their body art. Finally, he said, "My dad had the same tattoo. The chain is for protection and he used to say it was the unbroken unity of our family. His had my mom's first initial, M for Mary. Then the D for me." She traced the two links with her forefinger. "I had this inked when I was eighteen. He'd been dead for so long I barely remembered him, but I remembered that tattoo. I added the G for him. His name was Geoffrey."

"Was he a firefighter, too?"

"Military. My whole family's military. He was killed in Lebanon in 1983 when his barracks were bombed."

"I'm so sorry."

Dylan was staring at the ceiling. "He always used to say, 'No guts, no glory.' He was proud to serve his country."

She said, "But you didn't follow in his footsteps."

"Promised my mom I wouldn't."

Suddenly he flipped her so she was on her side facing away from him. He kissed the back of her neck and then his tongue began to trace the bumps of her spine. "You're so delicate for how strong you are."

She felt the glorious slide toward arousal as his right hand got busy with her front, stroking her sensitive breasts, tracing her ribs with his fingers even as his tongue traced the bones of her back. He stroked her belly, down between her legs until he found her most secret places.

A glorious weakness spilled over her as she gave herself over to his hands and his mouth and the rising tide of excitement.

He reached over and she heard a drawer open, then the familiar rustle and tear of a condom wrapper.

Heat rushed through her. Soon he'd be inside her again, and even though her body felt satiated and well used, she didn't think she could wait another second.

Not many seconds later she felt him nudge between her thighs, heavy and warm, finding her hot and ready. He entered her slowly, stretching and reaching, up, up to that magic spot. When he hit it she gasped.

He kept up the motion of his fingers working her clit and began to drive into her. She reached behind her, grabbing his hip with one hand, needing something to hang on to as he rocked them both up and up.

Sounds spilled out of her mouth, guttural words and cries as she bucked against him, driving them both higher.

He tossed her up and over the edge as effortlessly as he'd been doing all night and then as her cries subsided, he grabbed her hips and pumped, long, deep strokes that drove her up again until they both fell off the edge of the world.

As she settled against him, drowsing slowly back to sleep, it occurred to her that he'd managed to avoid a personal conversation in a very efficient way.

WHEN CASSIE WOKE again it was thanks to her alarm reminding her she had to go to work. She knew the instant her eyes opened that she was alone in bed. She rolled out slowly, feeling stretched and tender in the best possible way, realizing she'd gone far too long without that particular kind of workout.

She was smiling as she hit the shower, still smiling as she padded downstairs in her robe, her hair clinging to her head in wet curls.

The smell of coffee drew her to the kitchen, only to find no one there but the kitten, who mewled piteously, scampering up to Cassie, wrapping around her legs like a hazardous mink stole, and then prancing back to circle her empty food bowl.

"Coffee first," she grumbled.

The cat seemed disinclined to wait. Then Cassie spied the open cat food on the counter, which certainly hadn't been there last night. "Oh, you little faker," she cried, half laughing. "You already had breakfast."

But when she gazed down at the bundle of fur, who was rapidly losing her gaunt look, she softened and added a few more kibbles to the bowl.

Then she poured herself a mug of coffee. There was no note. What did that mean? Was Dylan coming back?

She picked up her phone. Then put it down again. She had no idea of the protocol now she'd slept with him. If she called would she sound like his employer wondering if he was planning to come in to work? Or would she sound like a needy sex partner checking up on her guy hours after he'd left her?

She picked up the kitten, who was purring so hard her small body vibrated, and carried her—and the coffee—out to the backyard. She settled on an Adirondack chair in the morning sun. This had already become a routine in the short time she'd been here, this early-morning coffee out in her yard with the cat curled on her lap.

"Is he coming today or what?" she asked the fur ball, who didn't seem to have an opinion one way or the other.

By the time she finished her mug of—excellent—coffee, she decided she was being ridiculous. Putting the cat down, so it brrped with unhappiness and stalked back into the kitchen, she followed and picked up the phone.

Dylan answered right away. "Hey, sexy," he said.

Okay. That was good.

"Hi. Are you coming by to work today?"

"Of course I'll be there. Why wouldn't I?"

I don't know. Because you slept with me and then sneaked out without a word? "You didn't leave a note. I wasn't sure."

"I left coffee."

"Is that some kind of man-speak?"

"No. It means I left coffee. I'm picking up some drywall. I'll be over in an hour or so."

"Okay if I paint tonight?" She wondered about drywall dust.

"Sweetheart, you can do whatever you want." He said it in such an intimate way that she felt herself blushing. Now that, she decided, was man-speak for *I had a great time last night.* At least she hoped it was.

"Okay. See you later."

WHEN CASSIE GOT into work she said to Lorena, the front office manager, "How's Arnold?"

"He's droopy, but they say he's getting better."

"Good. I need my star of the cephalopod tank back

in action." Arnold was a giant octopus who'd been mysteriously taken sick.

"You have bigger problems."

"Bigger than a giant octopus?" She couldn't imagine.

"Way bigger." Lorena passed her a note but explained the contents anyway. "Allison Morganstern's mother called. She's got mono." Allison was one of their teen ambassadors, a high-school student who was supposed to run a birthday party in the aquarium this coming Saturday night. Sleepover birthday parties in the aquarium were not only incredibly popular, but a nice money-making venture that helped support important work and hopefully raise a generation of kids sensitive to the plight of the aquatic environment.

Didn't mean that Cassie wanted to be stuck with twenty overexcited eight-year-olds on her day off, which was what would happen if she didn't find a replacement.

"Why didn't I go into hard science like I planned?"

"And why didn't I stay in the military?" Lorena replied. "I'd be a general by now. Or retired."

"Bad choices."

"You better start calling teenagers before we get started talking about men."

Cassie laughed. Even with sick octopi and teenagers, she loved her job and the people she worked with. Lorena might be grumpy on occasion, but she was passionate about the aquarium and all the creatures housed within it.

Cassie went to her desk, pulled up her directory of part-time party planners and started calling.

Of course, the kids who weren't home sick with mono or some other inconvenient disease were at school, so she talked to a couple of moms and left a few messages. It was all she could do.

About midmorning a call came in from Phil Daven-port, one of her diving buddies and an old boyfriend. "Phil," she said with pleasure when she heard his voice. "How are you?"

"Apart from nursing a broken heart since you dumped my very fine ass, I'm okay."

She chuckled. "Your very fine ass recovered fine. How are Marianne and the kids?"

Phil was as close as she'd ever come to marriage, and she'd considered it seriously when he'd proposed three years ago. They were good friends, both loved to dive and both had trained as marine biologists, though he'd gone on to become a doctor. But the truth was, they were meant to be friends, not a couple. She'd suf-fered a pang when he'd met and married a woman soon after they split up, but Marianne was perfect for him. She was a pediatrician who had recently given birth to twins. And Cassie spent the next few minutes listen-ing to stories of how hard life was with two newborns, though she wasn't fooled for a second. Phil was crazy about his three girls.

"But that's not why I called," he said after a while, when she was beginning to wonder if he was working up to ask her to babysit or something. "I was diving on the weekend." He named a remote area where few people other than divers ever went. "We pulled into a shallow cove to overnight on the boat and there was a single killer whale in there. A young one. I wouldn't have thought too much about it, but he cried all night."

"Is it wounded or sick?" Cassie grabbed a pad of paper and a pen and began making notes. The aquar-ium was part of a research project where they tracked the local pods. Each orca that frequented the area had a tag, a number and a name.

"Not that I could see. The whale didn't approach the boat, just seemed lost."

"Do you think it got separated from its pod?" Whales traveled in communities, so if one of the whales had got lost this was indeed news.

"This might sound stupid, but I think it's stuck. Seemed like it didn't want to cross the reef to get back out to sea."

"Is the orca still there?"

"Far as I know."

She got specific location coordinates for the cove and said, "Thanks, Phil. I'll keep you posted on this."

"Do. And you'll be getting an invitation to the girls' christening."

"Can't wait."

She grabbed a coffee and went into the back of the aquarium, where the scientists worked.

Three people were gathered around Earl Sandoval's computer. Earl was their chief marine biologist. Perfect. She joined the group. "I had a call from a diving friend," she said and relayed the conversation.

"Your diver friend thinks the whale is stuck?" Earl seemed skeptical.

"Phil and I trained together. If he hadn't switched to med school, he'd be a marine biologist by now. He also dives a lot. He understands the habits of sea creatures. I think he's credible."

Earl looked around at his crew. "Who wants to go on a boat ride?"

They had a fairly strict policy of noninterference, but they would want to check on the whale, ID it and then monitor its progress.

She walked back to her desk knowing she shouldn't worry about a whale, but unable to help herself. The large mammals were intelligent, they communicated—the baby would be lost without its family.

Maybe that's why she'd taken her marine-biology degree and gone into the community-relations part of the aquarium. She was better at warm and fuzzy science than cold, hard research.

She'd be part of the team heading out to check on the whale, and she'd talked with Earl about hiring a freelance cameraman who was working with her on a documentary film about the aquarium. This was a great opportunity for footage.

She couldn't stand the thought of a lonely animal of any kind. Maybe they couldn't pick the whale up and deliver it back, but perhaps they could nudge the poor thing in the right direction.

She had a momentary flash of Dylan, separated from his own pod. Now that he was on forced leave from his fire crew, she wondered if he was feeling lost.

Was that why he was suddenly sleeping with her?

She had a lost man, a lost kitten and a lost whale suddenly crowding her life. When had she become the patron saint of strays?

11

DYLAN WAS HAPPY to have Cassie's house to himself. Well, apart from the kitten, who was as nosy and intrusive as a building inspector.

This was a new one for him, sleeping with a client. Of course, he'd never had a client like Cassie, someone sweet and kind of funny and hot. He'd planned to keep his distance, but that hadn't gone too well. Now what? He liked her, he'd enjoyed the sex. No, the sex had pretty much rocked his world. But he didn't sleep with coworkers and he'd have said, if asked, that he didn't sleep with clients.

And there were good reasons for that. First, what the hell was he? Her employee? Her stud muffin?

"Shit," he exploded when he missed the nail he was banging into the pieces of fresh drywall he'd needed in the bathroom and nearly hit his own thumb. Already she was affecting him. His concentration was shot all to hell.

He'd take off early, make sure he was gone when she got home, and leave a note. Try to do most of his work when she wasn't around. Not because he didn't like her and want to have sex with her again, but because he didn't want either of them thinking this was anything more than it was.

That settled to his satisfaction, he got back to the drywall project. Sometimes, when Dylan was absorbed in a project, he fell into a kind of zone where time was a remote concept. It happened today. He got so caught up in the job that he was still taping drywall seams when the kitten suddenly deserted him and scampered away so fast that he stopped and listened. Sure enough, he heard the cooing of his employer and he could almost believe he heard the cat purr from here.

"Hey," he yelled.

Long, sexy legs in tight jeans entered his line of vision. "Hey, yourself."

He glanced up at her and all ideas of keeping his distance vanished like a popping soap bubble. He rose, wiped his dusty hands on even dustier jeans, and walked forward. She held the kitten in her arms and watched him come toward her, an expression in her eyes that made his old work pants suddenly feel tight. He led her out of the dust zone to the empty living room.

"How was your day?" he asked.

"Mixed. We've got a young adult male separated from his pod."

"Can you put him back?"

"Yes. But we won't. We try not to interfere with nature."

"Sucks for the whale."

"My thoughts exactly. And the teenager who is supposed to run a big birthday party caught mono."

He shook his head. Staring at her mouth. "Kissing disease. There's a lot of that going around."

She was so cute when she got that particular expression on her face, the amused but sexy one. He moved forward, tried not to touch her because of his dirt, simply reached forward and took her mouth with his.

"I need a shower," he said, pulling back, forcing himself not to crush her to him, dirt and all.

"You do."

"I made you purr."

She chuckled. The cat looked at him pointedly, seeming to be suggesting that if he got that close to Mom one more time he was going to get his eyes scratched out.

He kissed her again anyway. Even more deeply. Only stopping when the doorbell rang.

It was so unusual that they both pulled back and stared at each other. Cassie glanced out the front window, but whoever was at the door was currently invisible.

She walked to the door and for some reason he followed.

It was the neighbor lady at the door, holding a white piece of paper. "Hi," she said brightly.

"Hi," Cassie replied.

"I came to personally invite you to our Fourth of July neighborhood barbecue." Her beaming face took in both of them and he realized that she must have seen him and Cassie in a lip-lock through the living room window. No doubt she'd also noted that his truck was parked outside all night. She seemed like the vigilant type. A one-woman neighborhood watch.

"That's so nice of you, thanks," Cassie said.

"We're a real friendly bunch. Everybody usually brings something to share, but the details are all on the invite."

"I'll look forward to meeting my neighbors. Thanks again."

Cassie walked into the kitchen and pinned the invitation on a corkboard that was part of the original kitchen. Then she listened to her messages and turned to him, looking excited.

"The kitchen cabinets are in." The ones she'd chosen had been back-ordered.

"Great! I can put those in this weekend. It will take two people, but I've got a buddy who owes me a favor."

"Fantastic."

"But you know what that means."

She sighed and glanced around that butt-ugly kitchen as though she actually liked it. "Bye-bye, kitchen."

"Hello, takeout. I'll start demolishing tomorrow."

She closed her eyes briefly. "You did say it would get worse before it got better."

"I did."

"So, you want the tour of progress?" He showed her what he'd been up to every night when she got home from work. Why should today be any different?

"Yes, I do."

He showed her the bathroom, saving the best for last. "You can turn on the tap."

She put a hand to her chest as though he'd just handed her a big honking bouquet of roses. "Really?"

"Yep. Plumber was by earlier. It's all working perfectly."

She stepped forward. Turned on the tap. Water poured out exactly as it should. It felt good to see the happy look on her face. Maybe his real job was kind of in limbo, but at least in his temporary job he could please his boss.

She turned the tap off. Turned it on again. Glanced at him with her eyebrows raised. "That bathtub?"

He stepped back and motioned her toward the soaker tub. "Be my guest."

She turned on the tab and the *glub, glub* sounded like music. "I am very excited about this. I can't wait to have my first real, decadent bath in here."

"The shower's not finished yet. It's still waiting for the custom doors. And don't go too crazy until I get the drywall sealed and a couple of coats of paint on. But otherwise, you're good to go."

"It looks even better than I'd hoped."

"I aim to please."

She sent him a look that melted bone. "You do please."

He damn near swallowed his tongue. He should leave—he'd decided hours ago that he wasn't going to act different simply because they'd hooked up. But that was before Cassie had come home looking all hot and reminding him of how great last night had been. Besides, most nights he did stay late. Leaving as soon as she got here would be acting weird.

"So, about that takeout."

"What takeout?"

"I was thinking, if you want to order pizza, I'll finish up the taping in the downstairs bathroom, I'm almost done. Then I could help you paint the spare room upstairs." He knew it was next on her list since her parents were making noises about coming to visit.

"But—" She looked a little—what? Confused, uncertain, weirded out? "You're working so many hours. I should feel guilty."

"Not if you buy the pizza."

She laughed. "Deal."

"Besides, what will take you three hours will take the two of us together about an hour, tops."

"How do you figure that?"

"Because I'm a better, faster painter than you are."

She sighed. "So true."

"But you get better with every wall you paint. That's the beauty of home renovation. Once you learn how to do something, you own that knowledge. This is only your first house."

"My first house?" She looked as though she were watching the final, goriest scene in a horror movie.

"Think big. You never know. You could end up fixing up houses for a hobby. Like me." He only hoped it was still a hobby and he wasn't going to find himself so screwed over by his captain that he ended up fixing up houses for a living.

"I'm going upstairs to change."

"We paint first, then dinner?"

"Sounds good."

She put the cat down in the kitchen and poured food into her bowl, put down fresh water, then ran upstairs. He watched those sexy, strong legs all the way.

Crazy. He must be crazy.

But he was kind of looking forward to painting a room with Cassie. Teasing her until she laughed, planning all the ways he was going to make love to her, and all the places and positions he wanted to do it in.

And he was a very inventive man.

"WHAT DO YOU like on your pizza?" Cassie asked as she pulled out one of the local pizza flyers she'd obviously been collecting. She had a little smudge of paint on her cheek, the same soft yellow as the guest room.

"Everything you're having plus extra pepperoni."

"Okay."

"Mind if I take a shower?"

"I'd be devastated if you didn't."

He went outside to his truck, where his gym bag always contained a change of clothes and his toiletry kit. He was in the habit of hitting the gym first thing in the morning, then heading straight to Cassie's. He always had clean clothes, a razor, a toothbrush and deodorant on hand. He grabbed the bag, headed back into the house. He ran up the stairs, thinking he really needed to get that downstairs shower finished.

He stepped into the ugly pink bathtub in Cassie's en suite, knowing he would be tearing it out pretty soon. He washed his hair, lathered up and was letting the hot water pound down on him, washing the last of the dust and grit down the drain, when he felt movement behind him. He turned and there she was, naked and glorious.

"I thought you were ordering pizza."

"Won't be here for forty-five minutes."

"That's a shame," he said, and pulling her under the wet spray, he kissed her deeply and hungrily, the way he'd been thinking about kissing her all day.

He grabbed her shower gel, which was luckily green and had seaweed or something in it so it wasn't an insult to his manhood, and squeezed out a good dollop in his palm. He used the gel, rubbing it onto her breasts so thoroughly that she began to make noises in her throat that he was starting to love.

He washed her until she was so clean she could perform surgery. Naked.

Then she grabbed the gel. She wasn't as thorough as he was, only seemed interested in a couple of spots—his chest, his arms. And then she zeroed in on his cock until he finally grabbed her hand away. He wanted to plunge into her sweet, willing body, but of course he hadn't bought condoms into the shower with him.

The same thought seemed to strike her at the same time, for she kissed his mouth, then began to sink slowly before him, kissing her way down his chest and belly before taking him into her mouth.

He had to hold on to the ugly pink tiles to keep his balance as that woman made him mindless with her sweet, sassy mouth.

When they turned off the shower minutes later, he stepped out first, handing her a fluffy blue towel off the rack.

"Spare towels in the cupboard there," she said, pointing.

He nodded, grabbed a twin blue towel and dried off swiftly.

She was still drying her hair when he dashed out, raided the condom drawer and ran back in again.

The bathroom might be in need of updating, but it boasted a long counter and plenty of steamed-up mirror. By the time the doorbell rang with the pizza, they'd steamed it up even more.

12

"Hey, you're eating my half," Cassie complained as Dylan lifted a piece of pizza to his mouth. She'd ordered half the pizza with double peperoni and half with none, so it was easy to see somebody was pilfering.

He didn't seem a bit remorseful. "I ate all my side. You're too slow."

She shook her head at him. "You want another beer to go with my pizza?"

Even around a mouthful of food he could grin in the most endearing way. "Sure."

He'd been right, of course—painting the bedroom together had taken half the time and been twice the fun. Not to mention the after-work shower. Whew.

When she went back into the dining room, where her TV and couch were temporarily stashed until the living room was finished, she found Dylan answering his cell phone.

"Yeah, need a favor. I've got Cassie's cupboards to install on the weekend. Need a second pair of hands. You in?"

He snorted. "Tell me about it. Yeah, okay. I'll get the tux. I'll get it." She heard a male voice from the other end of the conversation, muffled but identifiable, then Dylan said, "Okay. See you at the game."

She stood there staring at him, the beer in her hand. "Did you just ask Adam to help install the cabinets?"

"Sure, he owes me some time. I helped him refinish his floors."

"But he's getting married."

"So not my problem."

"I—I can't believe this."

Dylan rose and took the Blue Moon craft beer out of her hand. "Don't think for one second he's not dying to poke his nose around here and see what I'm doing. He loves this stuff. Besides, he wants to make sure I'm doing a good job for you."

She still felt guilty stealing Adam away from his own renovation. Never mind any wedding planning. "Serena will kill me."

"I doubt it."

He sat back down and flipped on the TV. Naturally, HGTV came up, because that's all she watched these days. She waited for Dylan to flip to sports but he didn't. He watched the spiel as the married couple were told they'd be shown three homes in their budget, all of which needed renovation, and they'd have to make some choices.

She pulled out her own phone, called Serena.

When her friend answered she said, "I am so sorry. Dylan stole Adam to help him put in my kitchen cabinets. Honestly, I had no idea he was going to do that."

Serena said, "And I thank Dylan for stealing Adam. It's like every spare minute I am dealing with power tools and a man who finds electrical boxes sexy."

Adam yelled from somewhere, "I can hear you."

Serena ignored him. "So one day of peace will be heaven."

"Oh, good."

"Why don't you come over? While the boys are making loud banging noises and grunting and swearing in your kitchen, we'll have brunch or something."

"I think I'd feel guilty leaving."

"Go," Dylan said, still staring at the TV screen but obviously eavesdropping. "We'll have a man day. I'll get Max over here, too. He's not handy, but he can hold things."

She felt slighted. "I could hold things."

"Not in a manly way."

"Okay," she said to Serena. "Brunch is on. Dylan's going to ask Max, as well, so we can probably steal Claire. She's still in town."

"Good. I have something I want to ask you both."

"Okay."

She got off the phone. Settled beside Dylan on the couch. "You have a boy date, I have a girl date."

"Cool. Now see that kitchen backsplash?" He pointed to the TV. "What do you think?"

"I think it's ugly."

"Good. Me, too. I would never buy that house. You can see how cheaply it's put together."

She quickly caught up on the young couple and what they wanted—naturally, both had different priorities.

"Which do you think they'll choose?"

"She likes the old-fashioned one that needs lots of work but has the big yard. He wants the modern one with the smaller yard. He's worried about upkeep."

"Which would you choose?"

"The third one."

"Really? That's the one I like, too."

"Because you have excellent taste."

"No. Because I like the bones of the house. And you can tell it's been loved, somehow. Sure, it's outdated, but I bet the family that lived there was happy."

"I like the mature trees in back and the neighborhood's established. And it's well priced."

"But they won't pick that one."

"Not a chance."

"I bet they choose the modern one with the smaller yard."

He made a rude noise. "They'll get the Victorian because the women always get their way in these shows."

"You gonna put money on this sexist argument of yours?"

He sent her a steely eyed glare. Reached for his wallet. "Ten bucks says—" He flipped open the wallet, scanned the contents. "Five bucks says she gets her way."

He slapped the bill down.

"Okay. Five bucks."

"Where's your money, hustler?"

She got up and went to find her purse. "Here you go. Five bucks." She put her note on top of his.

"Ha," she said when her couple won. She scooped up the money with a flourish. "I am so much better at reading people than you are."

"You work with fish all day. That was a total fluke." He glanced at the TV and a smug look came over his face. "There's another episode playing right after this one. Double or nothing?"

She slapped the money back down. How did he make everything more fun? "Deal."

Dylan didn't mention going home to his place, and neither did she. After they'd broken even on their betting and watched the evening news like an old married couple, Dylan flipped off the TV. He turned to her, all sexy and warm and said, "You know, I had another idea for your bedroom."

"You did?"

"Yep. I had an idea that I'd like to see you naked in it in about thirty seconds."

And just like that, her arousal roared to full force. Again.

She crossed her arms in front of her. "Thirty seconds, huh?"

He glanced at his watch. "Twenty-five now. You'd better get going."

"Or what?"

"Or I'll have to do the job myself."

Talk about a no-lose proposition.

Still, it was kind of fun to run up the stairs as though hungry wild animals were after her and hear him come pounding up the stairs behind her.

As she ran she yanked pieces of clothing off and threw them behind her in his general direction.

"Fifteen," he yelled as he dodged a T-shirt.

She hopped in place to get one sock off, ran a couple of steps and stripped off the second. Lobbed them over her shoulder.

"Ten seconds."

"Your watch is fast," she yelled, giggling as she ran for her bedroom.

"Nine."

She was undoing her jeans.

"Eight."

Yanking them down. And off.

"Six." She tossed them on the floor. Down to panties and bra.

"Five."

She had the bra unhooked and as he entered the room she threw it at him.

He dodged. Not even looking at his watch anymore, his gaze glued to her body.

"Five." His voice sounded husky.

"You already said five."

"I'm giving you extra time."

So she took it. In five seconds, she slipped her panties down her legs, giving him a full view of everything she had.

"Time's up," he said, advancing on her slowly.

"Wait," she said, holding up a hand before he reached her. The air felt good on her naked skin. Probably because she was so aroused she was extra sensitive. Plus, there was the way Dylan was looking at her. Hungry. Aroused. Insatiable.

"What?"

"What do I get in return? I stripped in thirty seconds for you."

"Fair enough." He unstrapped his watch and handed it to her. "You can time me. I'll strip in thirty seconds, too."

She shook her head slowly.

"You don't want me naked?"

"Oh, I do, but not in thirty seconds."

He had his hands at the hem of his shirt, all ready to yank it over his head, but he paused. Raised his brows in a silent question.

She walked naked to the bed, pulled back the duvet and stacked a couple of pillows behind her. Then she sat down, stretched her legs out comfortably and consulted his watch. The strap was still warm from his skin.

She said, "I want you to strip for me. But I don't want any kind of rushing. I want it to last five minutes."

"Five minutes!" He gaped at her. "Why, in five minutes I could have you so—"

"Five minutes, and not one second sooner."

"You're asking for a damned striptease." Where he'd been more than happy to rip his clothes off in seconds, he was definitely hesitant about doing it slowly. Which made her more happy than she could believe. He was always so confident, so perfectly in tune with his body that it was fun to watch him toy with awkwardness for a moment.

He looked at her like a poker player trying to bluff a bad hand. "What if I promised you—"

"Five minutes. And the clock doesn't start until I see you begin to undress. Very slowly."

He scratched his head. "Can I have my watch back?"

"No." She bit her lip to stop from laughing. "But I could find you some music."

"You mean like in a peeler bar?" He sounded both petulant and into it.

"Exactly like in a peeler bar."

She picked up her iPod, flipped through her choices. Then smiled. "Oh, this is perfect."

She put the iPod into the dock and turned up the volume. Soon Beyoncé's voice boomed into the room.

"You have got to be kidding me. 'Single Ladies'?"

"Indeed." She glanced at his watch, then at him.

Dylan, she discovered, was a man who knew how to rise to the occasion. He sent her a glance that suggested he was going to make her pay. Then he started to move to the music. He gyrated, he twerked, he strutted, a cross between Mick Jagger and the great Beyoncé herself. He might have her hooting with encouragement and some giggles, but he still managed to arouse her. What that man could do with his body.

He raised his shirt slowly, teasing her with those abs that rippled as he gyrated his hips. Then he dropped the shirt back down, started on his pants. Seemed to change his mind. Coyly worked himself around until his scrumptious butt was facing her.

"Show me some skin," she yelled.

He went back to his shirt, peeling it off slowly so she saw his back emerge and she remembered how much she loved to run her hands up and down his back, how it stretched and rippled when they were making love. Off came the shirt. He turned with the music, twirled the shirt over his head, and she watched the dark inked chain on his bicep seeming to move with him. Then he tossed the shirt to her. She caught it, feeling its warmth, never taking her eyes off that spectacular body.

How he managed to take off his jeans so smoothly while simultaneously thrusting his pelvis back and forth was amazing. But he did it. Then he was left with nothing on but his briefs.

He preened, he thrust, he toyed with her. She couldn't take her eyes off the bulge in those briefs, or in fact all the parts of him working in harmony as he teased her, had fun with her, seduced her.

The song ended. He was naked.

She glanced at the watch. "You still have a minute," she said.

"If I Were a Boy" came on next. And for the next minute, Dylan, naked and fully aroused, showed her all the ways he was not a boy, but a man.

In the end, she forgot all about keeping time. She simply enjoyed this gorgeous, sexy, funny man and he walked over to her, leaned over and kissed her deeply.

Strangely, for all their earlier joking, their lovemaking was the most serious it had ever been. She felt that this meant something to both of them. Something deep and real.

They came together and he looked right into her eyes as they both climaxed, letting her see all of him, knowing he was seeing all of her.

Afterward, she curled up against him.

He played with her hair while they recovered their breath. After a bit, he said, "We need to get you a decent headboard."

"I'm looking for the perfect one, but I haven't found it yet."

"Make sure it's a good, solid four-poster."

Since he was very good at decor, and she hadn't been considering a four-poster bed, she raised her head to look at him. "Why?"

The devil lights were in his eyes. "So I can tie you up and spank you. Ever since *Fifty Shades of Grey,* my sources tell me that women want to be tied up and spanked."

"I don't want to be spanked."

"Just tied up, then. I can work with that."

She punched him on his tattoo. But even though he'd made her smile, she was a little disappointed. She'd thought, after the intimacy of their lovemaking, that he'd been about to say something significant. But she was beginning to realize that Dylan always went for the joke.

13

CASSIE SHOWED UP at Serena's luxury apartment a few days later for the promised brunch. "You're sure you don't mind me leaving you?" she'd asked Dylan one more time before she left.

"For the next few hours, this is a man-only zone," he'd assured her.

"Okay. Just don't get testosterone all over my new cabinets."

"When the counters are installed, the first thing I'm going to do is have you all over the cabinets."

"Do you ever think about anything but sex?"

"Not when you're around." Then he'd given her a deep kiss and sent her on her way.

Serena let her up and as she entered she was aware of what a calm, feminine refuge Serena's apartment was. There were no piles of boxes, no drop sheets, no drywall leaning against walls. No paint cans. Just rooms filled with light and soft furnishings, good art, soft music playing.

Serena accepted the cold bottle of champagne she'd brought with a "You didn't have to," and then immediately poured her a mimosa.

"So, how's the hot sex with Dylan?"

Her jaw fell open. "I can't believe he blabbed to Adam."

Serena laughed, completely delighted with herself. "He didn't. It was an educated guess, which you just confirmed."

"I wasn't ready to tell you."

"Honey, your face showed me when you walked in the door. You've got that freshly shagged look."

She ran to the mirror in the hallway and checked herself out. She had to admit there was a certain glow to her cheeks and eyes. Serena was nothing if not observant.

"Okay. So we had sex."

"Come on. You were dying to tell me. Before Claire gets here, tell me everything. Is Mr. June as good as he looks?"

Maybe she was ready to share the juicy details with someone who got it. "Better. Oh, so much better."

"As good as this champagne?" It was real French champagne, which Cassie had bought knowing Serena always surrounded herself with the best.

"As good as this champagne, and the finest selection of Godiva chocolate, and that pair of shoes you would run into a burning building to rescue."

"No man is that good."

Cassie just smiled.

But then, Serena had Adam, and you could tell by looking at them that those two burned up the sheets. She was about to comment when the intercom went.

"Claire," Serena said, going over to let their new friend in. Then she rose and prepared another mimosa, somehow robbing Cassie of the opportunity to confirm that everything was as wonderful in Serena and Adam's world as she was certain it was.

Claire had brought sunflowers. A big yellow bouquet of happy. Serena arranged the flowers in a long, elegant vase and placed it on the coffee table. The women sipped their drinks.

"It's so nice not to hear the constant roar of some power tool," Cassie said, enjoying the soft strains of classical music.

"Or the constant drone of airplanes," Claire agreed.

They chatted casually for a few minutes, then Serena put down her drink with a click.

She seemed a little tense.

"I'm really glad we could do this. I wanted to talk to you both." And then Cassie noticed that she wasn't as observant as her friend. If she'd looked closely, she'd have noticed the strain around Serena's eyes. The blue lines of a sleepless night.

"I've never had lots of female friends," Serena began. She sipped her drink. "I was a freak at school, the girl who studied like crazy and never had friends over because my trailer wasn't exactly comfortable, and my mother was as far from June Cleaver as you could get."

Cassie wondered if Serena even realized how far she'd come to be able to talk about this stuff.

"I'm not complaining, my mom did the best she could, but, well, I'm thirty-two and I realize that I've got a lot of acquaintances, but very few friends." She glanced at Claire. "Max is my friend. And the woman I work with is becoming a friend, but it's always been difficult for me to open up. To trust."

"I'm your friend," Cassie said. Because she could see how much Serena was putting herself out on a limb to admit how she felt.

"I don't know you very well, but I'd like to be your friend," Claire said, as though understanding instinctively that the woman hosting brunch in her elegant apartment was taking a risk.

Serena nodded, sending them both a grateful look.

"I was going to ask you both if you'd be my bridesmaids." She sent them a twisted smile. "Or best women. Adam has asked both Max and Dylan to be his best men and I realized I hadn't thought about having someone stand up with me."

Seemed an odd way to phrase the request. Cassie glanced at Claire and found her returning the glance, equally perplexed.

"I'd be honored," she finally said.

"Me, too," Claire echoed.

"Except the thing is, I'm not sure Adam and I are getting married."

DYLAN WAS HAPPY enough doing demolition—well, he'd loved making big noises and big messes ever since he was a kid knocking over a pile of blocks or blowing up stuff in video games. But as much as he enjoyed the messy, dirty, noisy demo in a renovation project, he was completely psyched to create a better home on top of the destruction. That's how he felt today as he and Adam and Max installed the cabinets in Cassie's kitchen.

He loved the richness of the espresso-finished wood. It would look fantastic with the cork floors and granite countertops. He hadn't been joking—the first activity those counters were going to see wasn't chopping vegetables for a stir fry. It was going to be Cassie, her sumptuous body laid out on those countertops for him to feast on.

"How are the wedding plans coming?" Max asked Adam.

There was a short pause. "We're having some problems," Adam finally admitted.

"Dude, if you want to know about the birds and the bees, you just ask," Dylan said.

Max shot him a look. Yeah, so he always defaulted to a joke. Sometimes it was better than getting into other people's personal stuff.

But he managed to keep his mouth shut as Max said, "You want to talk about it?"

Adam put down the level they were using to get the cabinets perfectly straight. "I worry about her, okay? I worry that the next guy who decides to stalk her will get her. That I won't be able to stop him."

Dylan knew how close Adam had come to losing Serena in the spring when a psychotic serial killer had stalked and nearly killed her. But how often in a life did that happen?

Adam wasn't being rational. Max knew it, he knew it, Adam probably knew it.

Then his mind flicked to how he'd felt when Cassie had announced she was going to join the team that would try and rescue the trapped whale. He understood that she loved to scuba dive and that she'd be out there in a small boat with a very large and possibly sick or deranged whale—and he'd felt a cold chill run over his spine. What if something happened to her?

And he wasn't in love with Cassie. Wasn't engaged to her. So he couldn't imagine how Adam felt.

THERE WAS STUNNED silence after Serena said she and Adam might not be getting married. Claire glanced at Cassie, obviously thinking she should do the asking since she'd known Serena longer.

The only problem was Cassie was so shocked she had no idea what to say. Serena was the person who always had the answer. She was the kind of woman you went to when life was wobbly and you weren't sure of your path. It was her life's work.

To have her looking as though she'd lost her own path was a bit of a shock. Like Martha Stewart suddenly asking for decorating advice. Or Julia Child asking how to bake a pie.

So, not knowing the right thing to say, Cassie plunged right in on the assumption that saying the wrong thing was better than this stunned silence.

"What happened?"

Serena let out a sigh that seemed as though she'd been hanging on to it for a while. "It started a while ago. I thought I was being followed."

"What?" Cassie's eyes widened. "And you didn't tell me? After you were stalked a few months ago by that crazy killer? You didn't think it was worth mentioning that you were being followed?"

"I did mention it," her friend said. "To Adam."

A bad feeling started under Cassie's breastbone. As if she'd eaten way too much hot sauce on an already spicy taco. "And?"

"He admitted that he'd been getting a few of his coworkers to drive by my home and office about the time I'd be leaving. He said he wanted to protect me, but, you know."

"It would have been nice to have the option to consent."

"Exactly. We had a fight. The following stopped."

"Well, that's good," Claire said. "He listened."

"Except that suddenly I'm getting all these texts from him. Which would be cute, except he's not a big texter. He was checking up on me."

Cassie recalled the day Serena had bought her the chandelier. They'd been standing outside and ogling the firefighter calendar when her friend had received a text from Adam. She remembered the look of frustration on Serena's face. And that she hadn't responded to the text. "That's been going on awhile."

Serena nodded.

"Did you talk to him?"

"You can't talk to Adam when he's in cop mode. He gives you this it's-for-your-own-good spiel as though I were in the witness-protection program. Yes, I had a bad experience in the spring. But the guy's in jail and he's not coming out. It's hard enough for me to get over those memories, but with Adam stalking me for my own safety, I can't move on."

"And neither can he," Claire said. As a woman who'd nearly been killed in a sabotaged plane recently, she had to know all about getting over terrifying experiences. How she'd ever gotten back behind the controls of a plane was amazing to Cassie.

"Have you thought about counseling?"

"Of course I have. Do you think Mr. Macho will sit down in front of a therapist and admit he's got a problem?" Her tone pretty much made an answer to that redundant.

"I am so sorry. I know he loves you."

"Even the six of us getting together after hockey practice on Monday was his idea."

"Maybe he wanted us all to socialize."

"Maybe. I don't even know anymore. But I can't live like this. I'm an independent woman. I can't spend my life in protective custody."

"What are you going to do?"

"I love him. But I don't know."

14

WHEN CASSIE PULLED into her driveway, she was happy to see that Dylan's truck was the only vehicle. She really didn't want to bump into Adam right now. She wouldn't be able to hide her dismay, or probably keep her mouth shut. Something had to be done, but she had no idea how to help two people she felt belonged together.

There was a slight frown on her face as she walked in, but even worrying about her friends couldn't keep the frown from flipping to a delighted gasp when she walked into the kitchen.

Dylan was putting the hardware on the cabinet doors, but he rose when he saw her. "What do you think?" he asked as though her squeals of delight weren't doing the talking for her.

"They look amazing. Better than I thought."

She danced around, pulling out drawers that slid with unobstructed ease, unlike the old wooden ones that stuck and shuddered their way open. If they felt like opening at all.

She'd gone for big pot drawers and already imagined herself cooking on the new stove that would be installed as soon as the counters were in.

The cupboards looked a little naked without the granite counters, but she had no trouble imagining how they'd look.

She ran to Dylan and hugged him. He swung her around, catching her delight.

"They look better than I thought, too," he admitted.

"Oh, I am so happy." She kissed him. "I love, love, love the cabinets. And I love you for giving me this kitchen."

The second the words were out of her mouth she wished she could suck them back in again. She hadn't meant to say she loved him. It wasn't like, *I love you,* she meant that—oh, crap. He was looking shell-shocked, as if she'd asked him to be her baby daddy, and she didn't have any idea how to clarify what she'd meant.

So she pulled out of his arms and opened all the doors she hadn't yet opened. Pulled out a few more drawers.

He dropped back to his knees and went back to screwing the stainless handles onto the door fronts.

"How was your brunch with the girls?"

She didn't speak for a moment. She felt the urge to tell Dylan about Serena's issues with Adam, but she squelched that impulse immediately. It wasn't her place to tell Dylan. If Adam had talked to his friends, and she hoped he had, perhaps they'd been able to knock some sense into him.

"It was very nice," she said at last. "She made eggs Benedict, only with smoked salmon, which has a fancy name that I've forgotten. They were fantastic. And we had champagne and orange juice, and—" oh, God, now she was babbling "—it was fun." She ended. Finally. "How was your work party?"

Again there was a short pause. "It was fine. Max isn't

much good for anything but holding things, though his math genius did come in handy when we were trying to fit the corner cupboards."

"I'm grateful to both of them. I hope you gave them a beer." She'd made sure she had a good stock on hand.

He glanced up. "They're both so whipped they had to run off back to their girlfriends."

"Poor baby. Do you want a beer?"

"It's not the same having beer with a girl."

She grinned down at him. "Okay, then. No beer for you."

She was about to ask him what he wanted to do for dinner. They'd spent every evening together all week, but suddenly she felt foolish. It was Saturday night. What if he had plans? They were working together every night when she got home. They'd order in or get sushi, and then they'd collapse on the couch and bet on HGTV episodes, then end up in bed together. It had become a routine in a very short time, but they'd never said anything that suggested their relationship was more than a convenience. What if he had other plans for his weekend? She didn't think he'd date anyone, not while he was sleeping with her—she instinctively knew he wasn't that tacky—but maybe he was planning a night out with the boys or something.

She had no idea what the protocol was.

"I bought new towels for the downstairs bathroom," she said. She'd painted it herself the night before while he'd been cleaning up the walls in the kitchen to get them ready for the new cupboards. She'd chosen the softest blue-green for the wall color and she'd picked out some towels she hoped would complement the color.

When she walked into the bathroom, she nearly dropped the towels. "What did you do?" she cried.

On the wall was a chunk of the original wallpaper, still stuck to the plaster backing. The mermaid riding her ocean steed, the whale or dolphin or whatever it was supposed to be. He'd finished the edges somehow and mounted the '50s mermaid on the wall.

"I can take it down if you want. I thought it looked cool."

She turned and threw her arms around him. "It is so cool. I love it, love it, love it. You are the best contractor ever." He had that magic touch of making something that was good so much better. The bathroom had been nice before, an elegant spa retreat, but now it was funky, it had personality. It had a pinup mermaid.

"You know what I was thinking?" His eyes got a sleepy, heavy look to them when he was about to proposition her, so she was fairly certain she did know what he was thinking.

"What were you thinking?"

"I was thinking we should try out that bathtub."

"Together?"

"Sure. It's a good-size soaker. Taps on the side, so it's perfect for two. Then, later, when we're all cleaned up, why don't I take you out for a nice meal? I've had enough of takeout."

He didn't have a night out with the boys planned. He wanted to spend his Saturday night with her. He was asking her on their first date.

"Sounds perfect."

She pushed down the shiny stainless lever that plugged the tub and started the fancy stainless taps she'd struggled for days to choose. So many choices. As the water gurgled into the tub and steam began to fill the air, he undressed her, and she undressed him. None of it took long.

Soon they were stepping naked into the bath. As they sank in, they came together, kissing, touching, making love like two sea creatures.

Later, when they were relaxing on either side of the tub, her legs resting on top of his, she said, looking at the mermaid on the wall, "I spend my life around water. And you're the opposite. You work with fire."

"Opposites attract."

"If I'm water and you're fire—" she splashed water at him "—that means I can put you out."

He rolled his body forward until he was on top of her. "Seems to me that fire warms water, even makes it boil." And oh, he knew how to bring her to the boil, all right.

She glanced up at him. He had water droplets on his eyelashes, and his hair was slick. "You don't think I could put you out?"

He seemed to think about this. "I think water can be used to contain fire, to stop it from burning out of control."

"You think a woman could control you?"

"Haven't met one yet."

And she wondered if that was because he ran at the first sign of commitment. You didn't get to be thirty-five and the proud winner of a Last Bachelor Standing bet and not be swift of foot where the opposite sex was concerned.

"I wonder if you ever will?" Her voice sounded almost sad.

He shrugged, sloshing water as he returned to his own side of the tub. "Why does it have to be about control?"

"Love should be two people making each other stronger, not one dominating the other."

"But it never works out that way. I always—" He stopped as his phone began to shrill. Since it was in his pocket, he reached his wet hand out of the tub and tugged his jeans toward him. "Adam," he said, then answered. "Hey, man. Cupboards are still standing. You're improving." Then his joking expression changed to serious. "She did what? Why?"

Her own phone began to ring at that moment. Since hers was still in her bag in the kitchen, she dragged herself out of the tub, dripping, and grabbed a towel. She'd have let her phone to go to voice mail except she didn't like the ominous sound of Dylan's short conversation with Adam. As she'd guessed, when she grabbed her phone, her wet feet slipping on the hardwood, it was Serena. "Serena, what's up?"

"We broke up," her friend wailed. "I didn't know who to call."

"I'm glad you called me. I'll come right over."

"No. I don't want him to find me here. Can I come over to your place?"

"Of course you can. Come right away. Bring a toothbrush. We'll drink way too much wine, trash men, and you can spend the night in my guest room."

She heard a sniffling sound and guessed her friend was crying. "Do you want me to come and get you?"

"No. I'll be fine."

"If you change your mind."

Another sniff. "Can Claire come?"

"Of course she can. We can have anybody you want."

"Just Claire."

"I'll call her right away."

When she got off the phone, Dylan appeared, naked and drying his hair with a towel. "Look, I gotta cancel our date."

"I know," she said. "Adam?"

He nodded. Gestured to the phone still in her hand. "Serena?"

"Yep."

"Shit. If those two can't make it, what hope is there for anyone?"

"We don't know they can't make it. Try and be positive, okay? He needs your support right now, not your commitmentphobe attitude."

"I'm not a commitmentphobe."

She stared at him. "You're thirty-five years old and you just won something called Last Bachelor Standing."

"Doesn't make me a commitmentphobe."

She snorted, following him up the stairs. He pulled on clean clothes, and she did the same.

She had no idea what he and Adam had planned for the evening, but she didn't think Serena would want to wake up tomorrow morning with Dylan in the house. She said, "Serena's coming over. I told her to stay the night."

He slowed his movements. Glanced at her. She thought she saw a hint of regret. "So I guess I should sleep at my own place, huh?"

"I guess."

He nodded. Grabbed his stuff, then suddenly came to her and pulled her into him for a long kiss. "You look after the bride. I'll take the groom."

"Shake some sense into him," she said, because she couldn't help herself.

He nodded. "Don't worry. I plan to."

"I really want this to work out," she said.

"I know you do." And as he left the room she wondered which couple she was really talking about.

15

In the end, Claire picked up Serena so they arrived together. Since Cassie didn't have a functioning kitchen, she didn't even think about cooking. She ordered pizzas and made sure there was plenty of wine and beer. She even had tequila and the makings of margaritas.

She considered pulling together a batch, but then worried that might seem too festive.

As soon as she took one look at Serena's face, she knew the problem was serious. Serena was always so calm and, well, serene. Cassie had always thought her friend was particularly well named, but not tonight. Tonight she looked half-wild. Her eyes were red and she'd obviously dressed in whatever was closest to hand, without her usual attention to detail.

A lot of women wore mismatched socks. Cassie herself had been known to semimatch a navy blue and a black because really, who had time for perfection? But Serena? Everything always matched, so to see her now, with one red plaid knee sock and one white athletic sock shoved in her Chanel flats, told the depth of her upset as clearly as the red-rimmed eyes.

"Wine, beer or tequila?"

"Wine."

Claire nodded agreement.

"White or red?"

"So don't care."

Wow. Second huge warning flag. Serena cared about stuff like that.

"We're having pizza, so I vote red."

Two answers of "fine" echoed from the living room. She pulled out one of the cabernets her dad had brought up for her from their favorite winery. She doubted Serena would even notice, but it seemed fitting to serve the poor woman a decent wine in honor of her heartbreak.

She poured three very large glasses. "Claire, you can stay the night, too."

"It's okay. I told Max we'd probably be drinking. He'll pick me up whenever I call him."

"Why can't I have a man like that?" Serena demanded. "A man who says, 'Call me whenever, I'll come and get you,' not a man who stalks me." Then she drank deeply of her wine. Like, chugged half the glass.

"Are we talking *stalking* stalking? Or more of that texting?"

"Ha." Serena pulled an object out of her pocket and slapped it on the table.

"What is it?" Cassie asked, though she was very much afraid she knew.

"It's a tracking device," Claire answered, looking concerned.

"Exactly. The bastard's been tracking my every move. When I told him to stop having cops tail me and I stopped answering every text, suddenly he plants a GPS on me. Two, in fact. One in my car, one in my purse."

"He did the same thing when that crazed killer was after you," Cassie had to remind her. "It saved your life."

"But I don't have a crazed killer after me anymore. Just a crazed boyfriend."

She noted Serena didn't call him her fiancé. *Oh, boy.*

"I'm guessing you confronted him?"

"Oh, yeah. This is the one I didn't throw at him."

Cassie rubbed her forehead with the heel of her hand. "I wish I could give advice like you do. If I were in your place, and you were in mine, you'd know exactly what to say."

"I'd say dump his crazed ass," Serena said, sucking back more wine.

"I'm not sure you would," Cassie said slowly. She'd been thinking about Adam's odd behavior ever since the brunch and she had the inkling of an idea. "The thing is, he nearly got killed, too, didn't he? I think you both suffered a terrible trauma. Everybody worried about you, and how you'd cope, and you healed amazingly well. But nobody ever worried about Adam. I mean, he's a cop, he risks his life all the time. But it's not his own life he's worried about. It's yours."

Serena put down her glass. She settled back and gazed at Cassie. "I was having such a good mad. Did you have to turn into a brilliant analyst quite so soon?"

Cassie was honored by the compliment. "I imagined I was you giving someone in your place advice, and that's what channeled."

Slowly, Serena sat back and no one spoke. It was obvious she was thinking, analyzing. Finally, she shook her head. "I can't believe I didn't see it. You're right. He's got some kind of post-traumatic stress disorder, probably."

"Which at least makes some sense of his crazy behavior."

"But he still has to get some help. Nobody can live with a man who's tracking her every move."

"No. They can't." But she thought it would be nice to have one who was a little more committed than one-day-at-a-time Dylan.

ADAM STARED MOODILY into his glass of draft as though the amber liquid had magic answers to all life's problems floating around in it. And wouldn't that be nice, Dylan reflected.

The clack of pool balls sounded from one of the tables behind them. He and Adam had been lowering the level of the pitcher pretty steadily, while Max was nursing his pint. He'd designated himself the driver for tonight's festivities, which was decent of him.

Adam had yet to explain why he'd called, except to say that Serena had dumped his ass.

Max stared at Adam for another minute then leaned forward and said, "If you cheated on her, I'm going to have to invite you out back to the alley." Max looked like a Latin playboy, and had been for a few years. But he wasn't soft. He might be shorter than the other two, but he was solid, all muscle, and he wasn't afraid to wade into the fray. He wouldn't be a bit intimidated by Adam's size, and if he had the moral high ground, well, Dylan didn't relish picking Adam up off the gravel. But Adam only shook his head sharply. "Of course I didn't cheat on her. She's the best thing that ever happened to me."

"We're agreed on that," Max said, relaxing somewhat but still hanging onto the pensive frown.

Finally, Dylan said, "Look, dude, we didn't come here to watch you stare at a pitcher of beer. We're your team. You tell us what's up, and we'll try and fix it."

He wasn't very good at pep talks—that was usually Adam's role—but the man was acting really strange.

At last Adam glanced up from his beer. He looked like he had after his first murder investigation: as though he wanted to puke and cry but he was holding it together because he was a tough guy and tough guys didn't puke and cry at gory murder.

"I put a GPS in her car and one in her purse. She found them and flipped out. Threw one of the transmitters in my face. Then she threw the ring at me."

"She threw your engagement ring back at you?" Dylan asked in amazement. This was more serious than he'd thought. As he was speaking, he heard Max say at the same time, "You were tracking her by GPS?"

Adam nodded yes to both questions. Then went back to staring at the beer pitcher.

Max spoke again. "Don't you trust her?"

"Of course I trust her. I'd trust Serena with my life. She's the most honest, decent person I've ever known. All she does is preach about the positive, bringing out the best in people. It's not only her job, it's who she is."

Max had a genius brain but even he looked confused. "What am I not getting? You trust her but you're tracking her movements?"

"It's not her I don't trust!" Adam all but exploded. "It's all the perps and pervs out there, the guys who'd want to hurt her. She's dealing with the public all the time. Traveling a lot on her own for business. I—I have to know she's safe." He sounded a bit out there, and Dylan glanced at Max to find him looking concerned.

"But you didn't tell her about the tracking device."

"She'd already flipped out when she found out I had a couple of buddies doing the odd drive-by to make sure she was okay."

Adam sipped his beer.

Max said, "You almost lost her once."

"You don't know how close it was. It was the GPS that told me where she was. He'd have killed her."

"He almost killed you," Dylan said, remembering what a close call it had been, a psycho kidnapping Serena, promising to teach her about fear, and her and Adam defeating the guy together, barely making it.

"I can't lose her," Adam said, his voice hoarse.

It looked to Dylan as though he already had lost her, so he kept his mouth shut.

Max didn't, though. "You will lose her, Adam, if you don't figure this out."

They all drank from their heavy glass mugs. Seemed the appropriate thing to do. This was one of their favorite bars. Dark, a little beat-up around the edges, where you could drink beer and play pool and hang out.

The music changed and suddenly Dylan heard Beyoncé singing about all the single ladies. It took him back to that foolish striptease he'd done for Cassie. He'd never forget the rapt expression on her face as she'd sat there, buck naked in bed, watching him. He'd been so excited he could hardly drag his grinding and bumping routine out long enough. He'd wanted to throw himself on top of her so badly, but then the longer he made them both wait, the more fun it would be when he finally tasted that hot woman and plunged deep into her responsive body. He shifted, getting hard only thinking about her. Wishing he was going back there tonight and not to his own lonely bed.

"It's not like I want to drive her away, but I know a world she has no idea about. I have to protect her."

In that moment Dylan had a rare epiphany. He saw himself running into that burning house after his captain had told him to stand down, ignoring an order, driven by an instinct stronger than discipline. "It's like you're compelled. Like you know better what's the right thing to do."

Adam stared at him, nodding. "Exactly. I can see a world she can't. Why can't she trust me?"

"Remember when I ran into the burning house to save that two-bit drug dealer?"

"Yeah."

"I thought I knew best, too. Almost got myself and another couple of firefighters killed." His brain felt clear and yet foggy at the same time. Even as he knew what he was saying was true, a part of him understood the instinctive need to protect, to rush in at any cost.

That recklessness had almost cost him his life, and his job was still up in the air.

A similar urge to protect was going to cost Adam his future wife if he wasn't very careful.

The waitress, a sexy blonde wearing a low-cut top, came up to their table. She also had a big smile and a friendly disposition. His favorite kind of waitress. "How you guys doing? Need another pitcher?"

"Sure."

She nodded. "Those ladies over at the table behind me were wondering if you guys are single."

He glanced over to find a giggling group who'd probably had more beer than was good for them. Seemed like a fun group of girls. He caught the eye of one, a redhead wearing tight jeans and killer boots.

"I'm engaged," Adam said, even though it wasn't technically true.

"I'm also engaged," Max said. But he pointed to Dylan. "He's the only single one."

"No," he said, almost without thinking. "I'm not single."

"Too bad," the waitress said, and he thought she wasn't only sorry for the table of giggling women.

Okay, so they were here because Adam had a monumental problem, but as the waitress moved away he found the two guys staring at him. "What?"

"Since when aren't you single?"

"I'm sort of seeing Cassie. It's no big deal."

"Define *sort of seeing?*"

He really wished he'd kept his mouth shut. "I've been spending some nights over at her place. She's terrific."

"I know she's terrific," Adam said, using the same tone he probably used when he told some perp to put his hands on his head and spread 'em. "She's not one of your playthings."

Dylan felt a rare spurt of anger. "Okay, I know you're hurting, but that is way out of line."

Max broke in smoothly, as though his two best buddies weren't leaning toward each other, snarling. "How many nights?"

Dylan narrowed his gaze another notch at Adam before turning to answer the question. "Pretty much every night."

"What are your intentions?" Max asked in that same smooth tone.

"What are you, her dad?" Sometimes Max was more Catholic than the pope.

"She's a nice woman. She's bought that house. She's going to want to settle down one day, maybe have kids. She deserves better than you."

"No, honestly, say what you really think."

"Two things," Adam said after a moment.

They both looked at him. And Dylan seriously hoped

he was going to go back to how he was messing up his own life. But no.

"One," Adam said, tapping an index finger with the other, "he's been sleeping with her for a week and he never said a word to me. Did he to you?" He glanced at Max and got a headshake.

"Two," Adam hit his middle finger, "he just told a table of hot women he's not interested."

"Oh, come on, I'm not an ass—"

"You think he's changing?" Max interrupted, turning to Adam.

Adam nodded. Grinned for the first time all evening. "I think our boy might finally be growing up."

16

CASSIE GOT A text from Dylan around eleven the next morning. It read, Is the coast clear?

She texted back, Yes.

Five minutes later he knocked on her door holding take-out lattes.

"How did you know how much I needed this?"

"Please. You had the bride. I had the groom, remember?"

"Yeah. Come in."

"Have you had breakfast?"

"I'm a woman with no countertops. I went out for breakfast. I took Serena. I think she's feeling a little calmer." The cat, hearing her favorite person in the world—depending on who was pouring food into her bowl and playing with her—wrapped her body around his legs, purring violently. He scooped her up. "Hey, Twinkletoes."

"You shouldn't name a cat you're planning to take to the shelter," she warned.

Dylan gave her a look. "I'm not planning to take this cat anywhere, am I, Twinkle?" The cat butted his chin and then curled over his shoulder like a stole. He could carry the cat like that for hours. She seemed to enjoy being hoisted on high and carried by a guy who was usually covered in dust and had a habit of making loud noises and a lot of mess.

"I'm surprised you're up if you had a night out with the boys."

"We had hockey practice at five a.m."

"Ouch."

"Yeah. Not our finest showing."

He glanced into the completely unfinished house. "Let's sit outside and ignore this for a while."

That sounded like a very good idea. Some days, it was all a bit overwhelming.

They carried the coffee through and out the back door. As they sat in the Adirondack chairs, she pictured the garden as it would be one day. When she had time. And energy. And a new infusion of cash.

"Okay," he said, "let's dish."

"What?" She couldn't believe he'd said that. He sounded like somebody on *The View*.

"Normally, I would not gossip about another man's shit. But obviously you know what's going on with Serena and I know what's going on with Adam. I say we share notes and see what we can do to get them back together."

She stared at him.

"What?"

"I thought you'd be the kind of guy who'd never get involved in somebody else's relationships, I guess." She kept her thoughts about him being a commitmentphobe to herself this time.

"Normally, I wouldn't. I figure it's their business. But Adam's my best friend. And Serena's the best thing that ever happened to him. I think he'll never be the same if we don't get them back together." He sipped his coffee, then obviously thinking he'd been serious for far too long—as in almost a minute—said, "Besides, I've already rented my tux for the wedding."

And she had a sneaking suspicion he'd look amazing in it. Okay, on her list of the many reasons why she also thought Serena and Adam should get back together, the notion of seeing Dylan dressed in formal wear noted a mention.

"A tux rental is a pretty big commitment," she agreed. The cat rolled over in Dylan's lap, presenting a white belly to be scratched. Dylan obliged without even seeming to notice he was doing it.

She understood how the cat felt. There was something about Dylan that made a girl want to offer him all her most vulnerable parts for his attention.

She sipped her own coffee. Brought her attention back to Adam and Serena.

"I missed you last night," he said in a low, sexy voice, almost as though he were thinking aloud.

And there went her attention, skittering away from Serena and Adam once again. "I missed you, too," she admitted.

Not that she'd been in the mood for sex, with Serena's broken heart in the guest bedroom and a few too many glasses of cabernet in her system, but she'd been aware of the wish for Dylan to be in her bed, simply for the warmth and comfort of his presence.

She knew these were dangerous thoughts. Dylan wasn't going to be permanent in her life any more than the stray cat. They were illusions of a life she might have someday.

"But right now we need to talk about Serena and Adam," she reminded them both.

"Okay. What do you think?"

"You know he's been stalking her every move, right?"

He winced at the term. "I know he's been a little overprotective."

"Dylan, he planted a GPS in her car and in her purse. That woman couldn't go to the bathroom without him knowing about it."

Dylan did a funny thing then. He reached for her hand. As he clasped hers she realized he'd never done that before. They'd had sex in every position in the Kama Sutra and a few more that they'd invented themselves. But they'd never held hands. She missed the first few words he said to her as she absorbed the feel of his skin, warm and dry against hers. His hands were, like the rest of him, strong, a little tough on the outside from hard work and firefighting, but also warm and resilient. She gazed at where their fingers joined. Her skin was so much paler and finer. Her hand so much smaller.

Then she heard the word *epiphany,* not the sort of word she'd associate with the good-time Dylan, and suddenly she was listening as intently as she'd ever listened to anyone.

His face was expressionless even as he scratched the purring creature in his lap and held her hand—he was far away in his own thoughts. "Maybe I have to go back. When we were kids, the three of us, we all had the 'what are you going to be when you grow up' stupid question thrust at us by well-meaning adults who thought it was adorable to laugh at a kid who wanted to drive the garbage truck or clean the pool or whatever fascinated our tiny brains."

He frowned. "But Max and Adam and I were different. We really knew, when we were little kids, what we wanted. I mean, who does that? Adam was going to be a cop because his dad was a cop and he idolized him. Max was going to be an astronaut, and believe me, he would have been if he didn't have bum ears. Max, he was a scary genius even back then. When me and Adam were making paper airplanes or those ones out of Popsicle sticks and busting a gut when they crashed into trees, Max was building model airplanes that actually flew."

He stopped for a second and she could see him tripping down memory lane. He grinned at her. "It was awesome. And if they crashed, he'd figure out why and make adjustments. Me, I always wanted to be a firefighter. I got this stupid red plastic hat for Christmas and I wore it everywhere. I had to take it off in school, and my mom made me take it off when we were eating, but otherwise I didn't take that thing off my head for probably a year. I knew that's what I was going to do."

She didn't entirely understand what this had to do with Adam and Serena, but it was fascinating getting this inside look at Dylan's view of his own past. He wasn't one to reminisce, so she had a strong feeling she'd better listen up before the trip down memory lane resulted in a dead end.

Somewhere in the neighborhood a lawn mower started up. But here in her garden it was peaceful. The sun warmed her, Dylan's hand warmed her. She had a strong feeling suddenly that everything was going to be okay. Her purchase of this house, her future. A guy she'd believed had the emotional depth of a puddle was showing so much more. It was one of those moments.

He continued, "I think there's something in people like us, almost like a sense of destiny. I don't think Adam did become a cop because of his dad. I think it's in his DNA to protect, to fight the bad guys and help the good guys. And trust me when I tell you he is the guy in the white hat. They don't come any better."

"But he's stalking her."

"No." He turned those deep blue eyes on her, as serious as she'd ever seen them. "I mean, yes, in a way he is, but it's not because he doesn't trust her. It's because he's so afraid of all those bad guys he knows are out there. It's because he is terrified to lose her."

She nodded. "You know what we girls thought?"

"No. What?"

"We think maybe he's suffering from post-traumatic stress disorder."

"PTSD?" He said it with scorn. "He hasn't been to war."

"Think about it. He didn't almost lose his own life, which I'm guessing he's made his peace with, seeing as he's a cop, but he almost lost Serena. After it happened, everyone was making sure she was okay. I'm pretty sure she had some counseling sessions."

He nodded.

"And I remember in the media how they were both touted as heroes. Well, they were. That was a seriously dangerous psycho they caught and put away." She still shuddered when she thought of that internationally wanted killer working as a trainer at a popular downtown gym. "And you remember what Adam said, every time he got trapped into saying something?"

"'I was just doing my job,'" Dylan said slowly.

"Exactly. Guys like Adam don't go to pieces because they are caught in a life-and-death situation. Or if they do, they hide it. Pretend it's nothing. That they're just doing their job."

"So what do we do?"

"If we're right—and believe me, when three smart women like Serena, Claire and me all agree, we're probably right—then he needs to get some therapy."

Dylan snorted. "Therapy? Adam's never going to get therapy. He's not some celebrity in L.A. He's a cop in Hunter, Washington."

"Then I think he might lose Serena. She can't stay if he's going to track her movements all the time. It's not healthy for either of them."

His hand squeezed hers. "I can talk to him."

"You know she loves him. She really wants to save their relationship."

He nodded. Started to withdraw his hand, but she held on. She had a strong instinct that if she ever wanted to know how Dylan ticked, this was her moment. She said, "About your epiphany. We ended up talking about Adam, but you didn't finish about you."

He blew out a breath. "Now I feel like I'm in therapy."

"It's very good for you. Think of it this way—I could be saving your future marriage."

He glanced at her and suddenly her mouth went dry. That's what happened when you spoke before thinking. You said stupid things that could sound like you wanted to marry the guy who was staring at you right now with a kind of question in his eyes and you felt your whole body wanting to yell *yes*.

It was as if an electric current sizzled through her body from her toes to her hair follicles. OMG! she silently texted herself. News flash. *You are in love with this man.*

He must have stopped petting the kitten, for, with a sudden and irritated brrp, the cat rose on her skinny legs, glared at Dylan and jumped down to go sniff in the garden.

The cat's desertion broke the moment, and she was able to breathe again. She'd save her own epiphany for later when she could think it through, but for now, she was still interested in anything Dylan wanted to share about himself.

"You really want to hear this?" he said.

"Yes."

"Okay. So, you know I've got all this free time to work on your house because I'm on leave from my job."

"Right."

"I had a slight concussion when the roof caved in as I was dragging a guy out of a burning house."

She couldn't stand the visual in her head, or the fact that Dylan could so easily have been killed.

"Thing is, my captain ordered me not to go in, but I went in anyway. I pretended I didn't hear him, but I did. And he's incredibly pissed off because not only did I almost not make it out but two other guys had to come in and drag me out."

She nodded. She knew part of the story from Adam, but she hadn't known the details.

Dylan's hand gripped hers, harder than before. She doubted he even realized he was doing it. "He says I'm rash. That I have a death wish."

"Do you?"

"No!" His hand spasmed. "I don't think so. Shit, I don't know."

"And this was your epiphany?"

"No. My epiphany was that sometimes you have an urge that's stronger than common sense or discipline. I think that's what Adam and I both have. We can't explain it, but we see it in other people. Max has it, too, only different. The three of us, the reason we've been friends ever since we were little kids is that there's something in us that we all understand. We're like those guys who serve together in a war, and even after, you always know those guys have your back. We never needed to go to war. We've always known that about each other."

"Wow."

"Yeah. So, this thing of Adam's, it's gone haywire and he needs to get it straightened out. And when I could see that last night, I started to see that mine might be haywire, too."

"That's an incredible insight."

He nodded. "I thought so, too. I have to do something about it or I'm going to lose my job."

"What are you going to do?"

"I'm going to see my mom."

She had to force herself not to laugh. It was the last response she'd expected. "Your mom?"

He looked directly into her eyes and she thought she could stare into them forever and never get bored. "Think about it. Every man in my family is military. Some of the women, too, but the tradition is super strong in the men. So why didn't I go into the military?"

"Why didn't you?"

"I don't know. That's why I want to ask my mom. Maybe she knows. Moms know everything."

Cassie thought about how when a really thorny problem came along, she was always glad her mother was on the other end of the phone. "It's true."

17

"HEY, MOM," DYLAN SAID, wrapping his mother in a hug. Sometimes he forgot how small she was. Or was she getting shorter? At sixty-two, his mother was as energetic as ever. She was the principal of the local school and a fierce tennis player. From the look of her white skirt and tennis shirt, that's where she'd been this morning. Her skin was tanned and her short hair still mostly blond, though there was more gray showing every year.

"Dylan, I was so glad you called. I think the garage door has something wrong with it. It's sticking."

"Okay, I'll check it out." Sometimes having skills as a handyman was not much of an asset. He didn't mind being his mom's jack-of-all-trades, but he got a little tired of fixing broken screen doors for aunts and uncles and being on speed dial for every cousin with a plumbing leak.

But the Crosses were a close clan and as Mary, his mom, always reminded him, the family had been there for the two of them when his father was killed. Being a military family, there were more casualties than in a regular clan. It made them close. Even when they were posted all over the place, the families kept in touch. It used to be a newsletter, but now it was Facebook and Instagram.

It only took thirty minutes and a little oil and he had the mechanism working perfectly. He made a mental note to add the garage door to his maintenance schedule.

Back inside the house, his mom was freshly showered and wearing a jean skirt and a purple shirt that showed off her strong shoulders. "Lookin' like a babe, Mom," he said, helping himself from the pitcher of lemonade in the fridge.

"Oh, honestly," she said, batting a hand at him, but he could see she was pleased. For a woman approaching retirement, he had to admit that she was a very nice-looking woman. He was always happy that she hadn't married again when he was a kid. He was pretty sure he'd have hated having a stepfather. But he was fairly certain she'd had a few discreet relationships after he got older. Which he thought was a good thing.

When he'd asked her once if she'd ever marry again, she'd said, "Your dad was the only man for me. He was the love of my life. Now it's you."

And the house he'd grown up in was pretty much a shrine to the two men in her life. His dad's photos were all over the place, his medals in a glass case in the living room along with the flag that had draped his casket.

The spaces that weren't taken up with photos of the late Captain Geoffrey Cross were filled with photos of Dylan at hockey camp, on the football field, at his grad, as a firefighter.

Even he could see there was no room for another man. Not in this house.

"Hilda and Steve invited me for pot roast for Sunday dinner tonight. You know they'd love to have you, or I can tell them I've got other plans and we can go out for dinner, just the two of us."

He knew she enjoyed the weekly visits to Geoffrey's brother's house. Besides, he hadn't seen his aunt and uncle for a while. "No, that's fine. We'll do pot roast."

She looked pleased. "I'll call and tell them to set another place."

While she was on the phone, he took his lemonade into the living room and perused the photos of his dad. He was studying one, a picture of his father holding a baby who was, of course, Dylan himself. His dad looked as proud as could be. He had his hair cut military short, and through the gap in his shirt Dylan could see his dog tags.

"Am I like him?" he asked as his mother came up behind him.

"So much like him I am amazed. Not to look at, really. You take after me more in looks. But your personality is very much his. He was a charmer, like you. Restless. Sometimes reckless." She smiled, put an arm around her son. "He was almost exactly the age you are now when he was killed."

A cold shiver crept up Dylan's spine.

In the couple of hours before they left for dinner, Dylan unclogged an upstairs drain and fixed a light fixture that was blinking in the bathroom. While he worked, he and his mom chatted. She told him a little about her work and her tennis. It was clear she had a full life.

"Do you ever get lonely?" he asked.

She stared at him. He wasn't usually one to ask personal questions. "I used to. When you first moved out, I would sit in your bedroom and cry." She shook her head. "Silly, when you were off living your life and I was so proud of you. But now? No. I've got the house to keep up, hobbies, a job I enjoy, friends."

"What about when you retire?"

"I imagine I'll do some volunteer work. Maybe run for the school board. And I'll travel. I might spend the winter months in Florida or California, somewhere I can play tennis when it's cold up here." She passed him a wrench. "You don't have to worry about me. I'll be fine."

THERE WERE NEVER fewer than a dozen people at Steve and Hilda's Sunday-night dinners. After Steve's protracted grace—which used to go on so long the food got cold until Hilda told him if he didn't speed them up she'd be serving cold cuts for Sunday dinners—the family fell to talking and eating. Often both at once.

Dylan was seated between his cousin Jeremy, who was on weekend leave from Whidbey Island, and his cousin Lorraine, a fighter pilot who was awaiting a new posting.

His uncle Steve was a retired air-force commander, so the talk was mostly military and politics.

Once they'd hashed over budget cuts to military spending and how the president should fix the Middle East, the apple pie was served up.

"So, Dylan," Uncle Steve boomed down the table. "I understand you were quite the hero. Rescued a man at risk to your own life."

There were a lot of things he could say to that but since he'd known Uncle Steve his whole life, he settled for, "Thank you, sir."

"That's right. You're a credit to this family. I said to your mom when you were dead set on being a fireman that it was a crime to see Geoffrey's son not follow in his footsteps, but when I heard about what you did, I was as proud as if you were my own son. It's the kind of thing Geoffrey would have done."

He lifted his glass of ice water in a toast. "No guts, no glory."

DYLAN DROVE BACK from his mom's, his mind like the roller coasters he used to love as a kid. It was whirling and swooping and sometimes taking his stomach along for the ride. This was what came of having a damned epiphany, he thought. No wonder he rarely bothered.

Still, he had a feeling that something life changing might be happening to him and there was one person whom he could talk to about it. He checked the clock on his truck's dash. It was almost ten. And Cassie had work in the morning.

Still. He called her on his Bluetooth, was relieved when she answered on the second ring. "Hope you weren't in bed."

"Nope. Watching our favorite show. And if you'd been here I'd have cleaned up. I've picked three winners in a row."

"You need to get a life."

She laughed. "Tell me about it. How was your mom?"

"My mom's great. Had dinner with the family. I was thinking, if it's not too late…"

She seemed to pick up all the things he wasn't saying. She answered, "It's not."

"I was hoping you'd say that. I'll be there in ten. Need me to pick up anything?"

"No."

It was only as he continued driving that he realized how that must have sounded. As if he lived there or something. *Oh, honey, can I pick up milk or bread?*

Sheesh. He'd better watch himself. She was a nice woman, and Max was right. A woman of—he realized he didn't know how old Cassie was. But a woman in her late twenties or early thirties didn't buy a three-bedroom house if she wasn't planning a family. She'd buy a condo if she planned to stay single.

But then, he'd bought houses, he reminded himself. Or was that different? Had to be.

When he got to the door he knocked, even though he had a key. He supposed after his offer to pick up her groceries or dry cleaning or whatever, he felt he needed to remind both of them that he didn't live here. He was visiting.

But when she opened the door, she looked so good that he couldn't help pulling her into his arms and kissing her, then whispering into her hair, "I missed you."

"I missed you, too." She glanced up at him, all cute and teasing. "I had to move furniture and boxes without my big, strong guy."

He picked up her hand, tested her bicep. "You can handle it. Besides, my mom had me working harder than you do. And all I got was pot roast."

"Oh, I can come up with something better than pot roast," she promised, and simply that certain tone in her voice, both teasing and seductive, had him hard as a rock.

He kissed her again. Wondered if he should lead her right up to bed and worry about his supposed epiphany later. But she was made of sterner stuff.

"Do you want a beer? Or a glass of wine?"

"Sure. Whatever you're having."

She sat him down in the dining room—cum everything room until the renos were done—and flipped off the TV. She returned in a minute with two glasses of red wine.

Then she sat beside him on the couch and turned her body so she could watch his face. "How did it go at your mother's?"

He took a sip of wine. Pondered. "I've barely had time to process this for myself, so what you're getting is raw data."

"Okay. I can work with that."

He found he needed to touch her, so he pulled her legs up so they were on top of his. Not the most romantic posture, maybe, but it helped to feel her warmth against him, feel the connection of their bodies touching.

She waited patiently for him to begin and he tried to figure out where to start.

Finally he said, "My dad was killed overseas when I was three or four. I don't even remember exactly. But I was little. I barely understood what was going on. You have to understand, my dad had been away a lot. He was a marine. He got sent on missions and we stayed behind. Probably, if he'd lived, we'd have been transferred all over the place, but that didn't happen." He took a breath. "Growing up, after he was killed, our house was basically a shrine to my dad. My mother used to tell me stories about how brave he was, and that my father was a hero. Other kids got fishing trips and a guy to go camping with on Father's Day, and I got a dead hero." He winced at his own words.

"Not that I had a crappy childhood or anything. I'm part of a big military family and we look after our own, but my whole life I heard how much of a hero my dad was. And how much like him I am."

"Aha," she said. He loved that he didn't have to spell

everything out for Cassie. She got it. Probably more than he was getting it himself at this point. His revelations were all so new.

"Yeah." He stared at the wine, deep red in his glass, and said, "My mom reminded me that my dad was about the age I am now when he was killed."

"I guess another *aha* would be redundant."

He nodded. "And then we had dinner with my uncle the retired fighter pilot and my cousins, and everybody's in the army or the air force or the navy, and we're talking military strategy and politics, and my uncle says how proud he is of me for the daring rescue. How I reminded him of my father. He raised his glass in a toast and said, 'No guts, no glory,' which is pretty much our family motto."

Her legs moved against his in a comforting way. "And you put it all together."

"I did. And I realized that I'm trying to live up to my dad's example. But the only way I can do that is to die a hero."

She reached over, took his glass from his hand and put it on the table. Then she took both his hands in hers and came closer until she was in kissing distance, but her eyes were serious. "Your mother doesn't want another dead hero."

"No."

"You have nothing to prove."

"No."

"I don't want a dead hero."

"No."

"I think I'm—"

And he kissed her, stopped her mouth before she could say anything more, force him to take in any more than he already had. He kissed her and let his mouth and body say all the things he couldn't say.

She melted against him, opening everywhere, every part of her. He felt it. Felt himself responding as he'd never done before.

They never made it to the bedroom. They made love on the couch, with the lights on and their eyes open. It was raw, searing, and when she came, when her body convulsed around him the way he loved, he felt a kind of wonder that he was here and she was his.

When she finally took his hand and led him up to bed, he felt lighter. A weight he hadn't realized he was carrying had been lifted.

He didn't know much about the wishes of the dead, or if they even had them, but he had a feeling that his dad, wherever he was, would have more respect for a son who fixed his mother's garage and made sure she was okay than some hothead who foolishly sacrificed his life to live up to an imagined ideal.

And even if he was wrong about his father's wishes, it didn't matter. Dylan knew what kind of son he wanted to be.

What kind of man.

18

WHEN CASSIE WOKE in the morning, she was alone in bed. She rolled out and put her feet on the floor. When she got downstairs, she smelled coffee and heard the sound of water running. She smiled hearing Dylan singing some horrible rap in the shower. She thought about joining him, but she didn't have time, and besides, the coffee smelled so good. With no counters, she'd had to put the coffeemaker on the stove top. He'd left her one of the mugs she'd refused to pack away, and the milk and sugar. She doctored her coffee, then carried it back upstairs to dress.

When she came down, Dylan was dressed, his hair damp and his own coffee in hand. "Good morning," he said, kissing her.

"Morning."

"Guess what day it is."

"The first day of the rest of my life?"

He was in such a good mood it was contagious. "The first day of the rest of your life with granite countertops."

"They're definitely coming today?"

"Already checked. They'll be delivered this morning. We should have them in by the time you get home from work."

"Which will be late. I've got operation whale rescue today."

"You know the first thing I'm going to do when those counters are installed?"

"Make me a gourmet feast?" A girl could hope.

He shook his head, coming closer, his voice as smooth as velvet. "I'm going to have you, buck naked on that countertop. You will be the gourmet feast."

At the involuntary sound she made, he stepped closer still, put a finger to the V of her white blouse, tracked the V so his fingertip grazed the top of her breasts. She felt her nipples harden, felt her heart speed up.

"I have to go. I'll be late."

He brought the finger up and chucked her chin. "You think about that all day. How I'm going to strip you naked and hoist you up onto that cool, smooth granite and lick every inch of your sweet, tasty body."

If she was already this aroused, he must be feeling pretty good, too. She let her hand drop, found the hard bulge in his jeans. Squeezed lightly. "We'll both think about it all day."

"Granite countertops," Cassie muttered.

"What?"

"The whale. His skin, the wet, dark skin with those white patches, it made me think of granite countertops."

Earl looked at her strangely. And no wonder. "Okay. What else do you see?"

Come on, she ordered herself. *Focus. Your sex life can wait.* And she was going to punish Dylan somehow for making her fantasize about those granite counters and what he was going to do to her on them.

Their boat had pulled up close, but not too close. The whale was still here, still making those sad sounds. The waves were small in this protected cove, but the whale still hadn't left. There were few food sources. Killer whales ate mainly seals and otters.

She stared at the whale, really studied the gorgeous creature. "He's got a slight depression behind the blowhole. Could indicate malnutrition. He's probably not eating. He's losing weight."

"Good."

Better than countertop comparisons, that was for sure.

"Rob, are you getting some good stuff?"

"Yep." The camera operator hung over the side, filming the whale as it breached and rolled, as it blew a spout of water droplets from its blowhole.

"I really hope this works," Cassie said to Earl.

"It's worth trying." After a long discussion, they'd decided to try luring the whale out of the harbor by playing recorded calls from its own pod. Hopefully, the juvenile whale's mother was one of the voices on the recording.

She watched, anxious and hopeful, as they waited for high tide, when it would be easiest for the whale to swim back out to sea.

The scientists set up and everyone held their breath. The whale sounds were eerie, haunting. Even recorded, it was a sound that called to something elemental in Cassie. She thought for a moment of the mermaid in her bathroom. She supposed if she could choose any mythical creature, she'd choose to be a mermaid.

At first, it seemed as though their whale was coming this way. *Come on, baby, come on,* she silently pleaded.

But Phil had been right. The whale got close to the edge and something made it turn back.

She and Earl exchanged troubled glances. It would die if it stayed in that cove.

She became aware of another motorized boat coming their way. Some sort of pleasure craft. She didn't pay it much mind, but Earl signaled and the other boat obligingly cut its engine. Perhaps thinking they were in distress.

They pulled close enough for Earl to ask for a favor, and tell the two men in the other boat exactly what he wanted them to do.

"What do you think, Harry?" one asked the other, who shrugged.

"Sure. We caught our limit so the fishing's over. Why not?"

The other, smaller boat buzzed into the cove. This was going to be tricky.

The tide was already beginning to ebb. They didn't have much time.

Once more Earl began playing the whale calls. Once more the young whale swam toward the cove's mouth, but this time, the fishing boat came behind it. The whale seemed to hesitate. "Come on, baby," Cassie cried aloud this time.

And all of a sudden, like a cork coming out of a bottle, the whale swam through the narrow opening back out into open sea.

A cheer went up from everybody on both boats.

She was already working on her media release, since everyone loved a good-news story. She made sure to get correct spelling of the names of the two men in the fishing boat.

As they all headed away, she went up to Earl. They

could see the whale already disappearing from view. "Will he make it?" she asked.

Earl put an arm around her shoulder. "We gave him freedom. The rest is up to him."

19

THE FOLLOWING SATURDAY, the three women sat together in a downtown restaurant where they were meeting for brunch at Serena's invitation. It was becoming a regular event. Cassie felt a little guilty about leaving Dylan, but he'd rented a sander to start refinishing the floors. He'd pretty much told her she was better off out of the house.

After the usual chitchat, Serena said, "The wedding's back on."

"That's wonderful." She knew Serena wouldn't have returned to the relationship if Adam hadn't faced up to his demons, and sure enough, she said, "Adam finally admitted he is having issues getting over what happened to me. I already knew he wasn't sleeping, but he says he's been having flashbacks and trouble concentrating. He's seeing a therapist, who is already helping. Plus, we decided to do couples counseling." She shrugged. "I guess if you start working on your problems before you get married, you're going to have an easier time once that knot is tied."

"And you're sure?"

"I'm sure I love him and I believe in him. Yeah. I think we're going to be okay. No more overprotective behavior. I told him I'm going away for the weekend before we get married. He started to ask where and then stopped himself. He said, 'Okay, have fun.'"

"That's real progress."

"I'm so happy," Claire agreed.

"It really is true that problems are a lot more manageable if you share them."

"Had you canceled the venue?" She knew that Serena had lucked out on a cancellation at a gorgeous historic mansion that offered private functions. If she'd given that up, her choices at this point would be limited.

"No. Luckily I hadn't canceled anything. The only problem is that if you two still agree to be my best women, then we're going to have to get dresses off the rack."

Since Cassie had never bought anything that wasn't off the rack—quite often the sale rack—and she doubted Claire had either, she felt comfortable teasing her friend. "Sorry," she said. "That's not going to work for me. Without a custom gown I couldn't possibly be seen at your wedding."

"And the handmade shoes to match," Claire added with mock seriousness.

Serena had a great laugh. And it was nice to see her looking relaxed and happy again.

They agreed that the three of them would go shopping together as soon as they finished brunch and find two matching dresses that all three of them liked. She was so happy the wedding was back on, Cassie vowed that she'd pretend to like anything Serena wanted.

Except, perhaps, a bustle.

Friendship only went so far.

But this was friendship of the best kind.

As she tackled her spinach omelet she said, "Okay.

Now that Serena's all sorted out, I have a problem. And I would like to share it with both of you."

"Thank you. It will be nice for me not to feel like the freak for a while."

"I'll sit in the freak chair." She drew in a breath, knowing that once she said the words she couldn't unsay them. "I'm in love with Dylan."

The chandelier didn't fall down from the ceiling. The waiters did not drop all their trays in unison, and the espresso machine continued to steam. Claire and Serena continued to regard her.

She glanced from one to the other. "Well?"

"That's it? That's your problem?"

"Yes."

"This is not news. You've been going around with a glow all over you. You might as well carry a sign that says, I'm in Love."

Cassie put her head in her hands, messing up her hair, which was never far from messed anyway. "But it's a disaster. I mean, look at me. I'm a normal woman who doesn't work out as often as she should, forgets to get regular manicures and my beauty routine—well, I don't really have one. And he's Mr. June. Hundreds of women in Hunter probably leave their calendars on June all year."

The two other women exchanged a glance that she caught. "What?"

Claire said, "I hate to break it to you, but it's on the internet, too."

"Oh, great. Dylan's abs are on the internet for any woman to ogle."

"They've kind of gone viral," Serena said with a grin.

Claire nodded. "My new accountant in Alaska has Dylan's calendar photo as her screen saver."

"Alaska? His abs are in Alaska?" Oh, this could not be good news for her love-struck self.

"Honey, Dylan probably has the most downloaded abs on the planet right now. I'm sure it's doing wonders for local charity."

"And I'm sure it's not hurting his already large ego, either." She put her head back in her hands. She might as well just leave it there. "It's worse than I thought. It's hopeless."

After a moment Claire said gently, "Is there any chance he loves you back?"

She raised her head. "Mr. Global Abs? Women from Hunter to Mumbai are drooling over him. What do you think?" Then she cried out in frustration, "Why him? There are tons of firefighters posing for calendars all over the world. Why is Dylan the one who goes viral?"

Claire glanced at Serena, who they both knew had her calendar open to Mr. June. Well, it *was* June, but she'd already admitted that in her apartment it was always June. She leaned in and tried to explain. "You know how Hugh Jackman ends up taking off his shirt in every single movie he appears in? This is kind of the same thing."

Cassie stared at her. "You're saying I'm in love with the Hugh Jackman of firefighters?"

"Pretty much."

"It's hopeless."

"He seems like deep down he's a good man," Claire said. "What if you tell him how you feel?"

"I don't know. I'm scared if I do that I'll ruin what we have. I know he has feelings for me. I don't know how strong they are. The one time I tried to say the words he cut me off. By kissing me. Like he knew what I was going to say and didn't want to hear it."

Serena said, "You might think about waiting until your house is done." When they both stared at her, she said, "I'm thinking it could be pretty awkward having him work on the house if for any reason he doesn't return your affection."

Cassie appreciated that Serena could be so practical. And she was right. The only thing worse than life without Dylan would be life without Dylan in a half-renovated house.

Although she couldn't imagine her house without Dylan. He'd put in the bathroom and was working on the kitchen. How could she go into the bathroom and not think of him when that '50s mermaid flirted from the wall? How could she go into the living room and not see him whistling while he pulled up that dirty shag carpet, revealing the gorgeous floors and gorgeous bits of himself when his T-shirt came untucked?

The kitchen? She'd have to change the countertops. She could never enter it without thinking of the night she'd come home after the whale rescue and he'd been waiting for her. He'd ordered in dinner. And there were candles.

And he'd spread her out on that counter and feasted on her exactly as he'd promised. The countertop had been cold and hard under her but that only seemed to add to the heat and softness of his mouth on her.

Her bedroom? When she thought of all they'd shared together in that bedroom, well, she'd have to move down the hall.

The truth was, she'd fallen in love with the house in the same way she'd fallen in love with Dylan. They went together in her mind.

All she was going to be left with was Twinkle. The one burden in all of this she hadn't wanted, but who was

wound around her heart now the way she wound herself around her legs when she came home from work.

She could see her future stretch before her. She'd
become the eccentric cat lady. The stray-cat network
would put out a bulletin that she was an easy touch.
She'd end up filling her empty house and heart with
cats.

Spend her life savings on catnip and be found days
after she died with a litter of newborn kittens in the
folds of her baggy black clothes.

While Dylan, of the world-famous abs, would go on
to be the next Arnold Schwarzenegger.

20

THE BRIDESMAID DRESSES—or best women dresses, as Serena insisted on calling them—were surprisingly easy to find. They went into an upscale boutique where the manager knew Serena and immediately fussed over her. Once she understood what they wanted, she took them straight to a rack of evening and party wear. They settled immediately on Serena's first choice. The matching dresses were a simple sheath design that fit where it touched. Devastatingly elegant and in a sophisticated blue. The kind of dress that a woman might actually wear again.

Of course, Serena still marched them to her dressmaker, who made a few tweaks so the dresses fit so perfectly they might as well have been custom-made.

Serena and Adam's wedding day dawned as perfect as a day ordered by the ever-efficient Serena could be. Not a cloud in the sky, but a slight breeze so the air was fresh and cool enough that Cassie could rely on her makeup and hair to stay in place.

The three women all convened early at the old Parker Mansion, a heritage home that was a popular wedding venue. Built at the turn of the century by a lumber baron, the mansion boasted a ballroom, a huge dining room and enough verandas to host everyone outdoors even in a rainstorm.

With no rainstorm in sight, however, plan A went ahead: a gazebo hung with garlands sat in the center of the lawn in the back garden. Adam and Serena had tried to keep the wedding small, but they were both popular people and while he had more family and friends, she had more business associates she needed to include. In the end, they'd managed to keep the guest list at a little over a hundred people. Which seemed huge when you were contemplating walking down a grass aisle in heels in the glare of one hundred–plus pairs of eyes.

She and Dylan had spent a rare night apart last night. He and Adam and Max had gone fishing together yesterday and finished up late. He'd assured her the massive drinking had all been done at the stag and this was "the guys hanging out," which she took to mean male bonding among males who wouldn't be caught dead using terms like *male bonding*.

Serena was a calm bride, but there was a sparkle of excitement in her eyes that was impossible to ignore. She looked happier than Cassie had ever seen her. She knew Adam and Serena were still working through the trauma and resulting issues from her kidnapping, but she also knew that they were both committed to making their marriage work.

In the upstairs bedroom where the three women gathered there were two hairstylists, a makeup artist and a manicurist, so there didn't seem to be a minute that they weren't being primped and beautified.

Cassie's normal beauty routine was a comb through her hair, a plastic clip to hold the mess out of her face if she didn't have time to bother and a swipe of lip gloss. Maybe mascara if she felt the need.

So to have a woman spend almost an hour on her face was a shock. Not to mention boring.

However, she had to admit that she barely recognized herself when she caught a look at herself in the mirror after her hair and makeup were done. Her eyes seemed much bigger than normal, her lips plumper. Her hair, upswept and threaded with pearls, was like something out of a magazine.

"You look hot," Artemis, the stylist, said.

"Thanks. If you and your team could move into my house I could look like this every day."

"If I had a dollar for every woman who's said that to me over the years I'd be—" he thought for a minute "—even richer than I already am."

She chuckled. "Did Serena coach you to talk like that?"

He smiled, and all his Greek charm came through. "No. She coached me to believe in myself and make a success of my business. The money, I made that myself. You should listen to that woman. She's smart."

"I know." As though realizing she was being discussed, Serena glanced toward them. Cassie might look hot, but Serena was beautiful. Her black hair shone like a starry night; the simple white dress showed off her perfect features. And she was glowing from within.

"You are the pearl beyond price," Artemis told Serena, and raising her hand, he kissed it. He said something in Greek, then said, "I wish you a perfect life of happiness."

Serena flapped her hands. "Don't let me tear up, or I'll ruin all your hard work."

"No! No!" he yelled. "Think of something sad. Plantar warts."

Serena blinked away the moisture. "Plantar warts?"

"It was all I could come up with in the heat of the moment. My mother suffers with them. It's terrible." He grinned at the bride. "But it worked. No more tears until all the photographs are over."

"Then I can cry?"

"Sob your heart out."

Before Cassie could believe it, the moment arrived. The three women hugged quickly. She thought Claire and she must share a similar beauty routine, because the other bridesmaid's transformation was equally amazing. She imagined Max would quite like his very sexy-looking bride-to-be.

And Dylan? She could only hope the man with the worldwide ab fame would notice her.

In fact, it would be fair to say that he did notice her. The three men were already standing at the gazebo, the chairs filled with friends and family of the bride and groom.

They'd tossed a coin to see which of the best women would walk up the aisle first. Cassie had lost and so had to be the first one up the lumpy grass in heels. As she began her seemingly endless walk up that aisle, Dylan stared at her as though he couldn't look away. The expression on his face, stunned and proud, was—gratifying. He didn't look as though he'd never seen her before—more as though he was enjoying seeing her at her prettiest.

She found his obvious admiration gave her enough confidence that she forgot to worry about falling off her heels and getting grass stains all over her expensive bridesmaid's dress, not to mention making a complete fool of herself. She focused instead on enjoying being part of the wedding of a couple she loved.

Adam was serious and seriously gorgeous in his black tux, but next to him, she thought that Dylan looked like one of those rough, tough action stars who show up at the Oscars in black tie and you barely recognize them. He was still his stunning self, but even the tux couldn't hide the muscles in his torso, and his hair somehow still managed to seem a little bit mussed, his air rakish. As if he'd been making out with a swimsuit model right before heading to the altar.

The wedding itself was lovely. Serena and Adam exchanged vows in heartfelt tones that brought a lump to Cassie's throat. When the minister announced, "You may kiss the bride," she found herself glancing at Dylan and caught his gaze on her, looking hungry.

After the ceremony, there were photographs, and it was understood she'd stand with Dylan as her partner. But he wasn't her real partner, not like Adam was Serena's and Max was Claire's. And she wanted him to be. She wanted to be with Dylan, she realized, to live in the house they were creating together, to have children with him. Maybe a dog to go with the cat that she was so clearly never going to take to a shelter.

Claire and Serena had gone to hell and back before ending up with the men of their dreams. Couldn't she work up the courage to tell her man that she loved him?

All through the delicious dinner and the champagne toasts she kept a smile on her lips and took her part in the festivities. But behind her smile her brain reeled.

Did he love her? When she caught him glancing at her, she believed he did. When she recalled their recent lovemaking she knew that something had changed. Ever since he'd come home from his visit to his family she'd sensed a difference. He was more caring; he seemed to tell her with his body all the things he didn't say in words.

But it wasn't enough. She wanted the words and everything that went with the words. She wanted her relationship with Dylan to be real and lasting, not a fling with a hot guy in a charity calendar.

The big ballroom was all set up for dancing and the live band was playing "Blue Moon" for Serena and Adam's first waltz.

Then the general dancing began and Dylan led her onto the floor and pulled her into his arms.

"You look so hot," he said into her ear. "I can't wait to get you home and slip you out of that dress."

Okay, that was nice, but she'd been hoping for something a little more meaningful. He'd been sending her soulful looks all night. Were they really only about getting her into bed?

21

WHEN THEY GOT back to her place, he didn't try to rush her to bed, which was unusual. It seemed as though Dylan wanted to talk. Her heart began to thud. Maybe she'd been right and the wedding ceremony had affected him the same way it had affected her, by making him see, as she so clearly did, that they were right for each other. Loved each other.

"I'm going to make some herbal tea in my beautiful new kitchen. Do you want some?"

His tie was long gone and he shrugged the tuxedo jacket off. Followed her to the kitchen in his shirt-sleeves. "Sure, that would be great."

She didn't know why she was making tea. She didn't really want it, but she wanted to postpone this moment she'd longed for her whole life, when the man she wanted to spend her life with told her he felt the same way. She was glad they were dressed formally. Well, semiformally now for Dylan, because this was the kind of conversation that you'd always remember where it happened, what you were wearing, what you both said.

Maybe the ceremony of tea would help make it that much more special.

He fussed around behind her, running his thumb along the seam of the granite, seeming to check the quality of his own work and that of the tradespeople he'd hired.

When the kettle boiled, she put chamomile tea bags in two pottery coffee mugs, poured the water over them and added a touch of honey. She didn't have to ask Dylan—she already knew how he liked his chamomile tea. And she knew how he liked his coffee. And his eggs.

She knew how he liked to sleep, his body spooned around hers and their hands clasped.

She knew that he liked his shower hotter than she did and that he took an extralong time because he always liked to finish whatever song he was singing. Unless he forgot the words—then he'd sing, "La, la, la," for a while.

She knew the places he was ticklish and the places where her touch would bring him to his knees.

He knew most of the same things about her. All those little and not-so-little things that summed up intimacy, his likes, his quirks, his moods, even his sneaky vanity about his body. They only made her love him more.

But did he feel the same way? Did he love the cute way she always rolled up the toothpaste tube so it was tidy and every last goop of toothpaste squeezed out so none was wasted, or did he consider her an anal, retentive cheapskate?

Did he like the fact that most days her personal care routine took less time than his? Or did he think she was careless of her appearance?

All of it, all the crazy-making wondering was really about one single question.

Did Dylan love her?

Finally, the tea was poured. He'd hoisted himself onto one of the barstools in front of her granite breakfast bar, so she sat beside him. Perhaps it wasn't the romantic spot she'd pictured, but the kitchen was one of the only finished rooms in the house, and it was gorgeous.

The mugs clicked on the new countertops.

He waited until she was settled and then said, "There's something I want to tell you."

She kept her face calm but inside her entire nervous system was yelling, *yes, yes, yes!*

"Okay," she said, hoping her expression was so warm and open that he'd have no trouble sharing his feelings.

But he wasn't looking in her face, so he didn't see how open and warm she looked. He was fiddling with his mug. "I went to see my boss yesterday."

"You did." Okay, not what she'd thought he was going to say, but obviously a man about to tell a woman he loved her might want her to know he had a job. Not that this particular woman cared that much. She already knew that Dylan would never sit around idly, and he had so many skills that if he gave up firefighting, he could take up property renovation. In fact, he was good-looking and personable enough that she could imagine him with his own HGTV show. Still, she nodded. "And how did it go?"

"Pretty well. I'd say very well. We sat and talked for a long while. I opened up about my dad and my upbringing and how I can see why sometimes I take stupid risks."

"That's really good. It must have been hard for you to tell your boss those things."

"It started out feeling like I was strangling, but after a while it got easier. He told me a few things I didn't know about him, and, well, he's letting me come back."

"When?"

He took a sip of tea that must have burned his tongue, for he winced. "Next week."

In the silence she could hear a car pass her house. Somewhere a dog barked. "So soon."

"Yeah. I'm really sorry not to be able to keep working full-time. I want to finish this job, but it means I'll be slower, obviously. I'll have to work around my fire-fighting schedule."

"Of course, I understand."

But she didn't, not really.

"Chaz broke his leg, so we're shorthanded."

"Chaz?" She felt as if she'd wandered into the wrong conversation. Who the hell was Chaz?

"He's a buddy of mine. Another firefighter. He broke his leg."

"In a fire?"

"No. Waterskiing. At least now Len Butcher has somebody he's more pissed at than me. Takes some of the pressure off."

"Well, that's good." But she was lying. It wasn't good. None of it was good. She put her hands around her tea, wondering how this conversation had veered so far from where she'd thought it was going.

"Look, I'll spend every spare second over here. I've got some guys I can hire to work with me. We'll get this done as soon as we can. I promise."

"And what about then?"

He stared at her, seeming totally confused by the question. "Then? What?"

A great calmness had come over her. She felt as though she understood that this night was a crossroad for her. "After the house is renovated. What happens then?"

"Is this a trick question?"

"No. I mean, what happens to us?" She didn't like the tiny waver she heard in her voice and that she really hoped he couldn't hear.

"Nothing happens to us. I mean, it's great, right? Why mess with success?" He sent her the charming grin that always made her weak at the knees, but this time it didn't. This time she felt as if he was posing, the way he'd posed for that damned calendar photo. Give the ladies what they want.

She could stop now, she could grin back and say something sexy and they'd be naked in a minute or two, they'd go on as they had every day since the first time they'd made love.

But she knew she couldn't. For some reason today had changed her. She'd helped two people close to her with their epiphanies, and now it seemed she was having her own.

She took a deep breath. "You know how your problem is that you're too rash? You rush into burning buildings first and think about the consequences later?"

"Un-huh. But I'm working on that."

"Well, my problem is the opposite. Sometimes I don't say what's important to me because I don't want to rock the boat, because I'm a pleaser. Because I'm terrified of rejection." Wow, even saying those things out loud was frightening.

She lifted her mug. Sipped her tea. Chamomile was supposed to be calming, but she figured she'd need a whole vat of the stuff to feel anywhere near calm.

"But I'm beginning to see that I need to start asking for what I want." She looked at him, could see the wary expression on his face. "And what I want is you."

Another pause ticked by, endlessly. "You have me."

"Dylan, I'm trying to say I love you."

He didn't exactly flinch when she said the words, but he didn't break out the champagne, either. In fact, he didn't react at all.

Okay, if she was going to be brave, to start turning into the woman she wanted to be, now was a good time to start.

She continued. "I watched Serena and Adam today tell the whole world how they felt about each other. I watched them commit their lives to each other, and I knew that's what I want. And I want it with you." Oh, Lord, she hadn't meant to blab herself all the way to a marriage proposal.

He reached over and took her hand. His was warm and strong while she suspected hers was sweaty and trembling. "Why do we have to rush things? Isn't it fine as it is? We have fun. Let's see where it goes."

Her jaw dropped so suddenly she was surprised she didn't bang her chin on the new granite counter. "I tell you I love you and your answer is that we have fun? This is what I mean to you? A few giggles and some easy sex?"

"No. I don't see the big rush, is all. So we went to a wedding. Weddings always make women crazy." He said this as though he'd been to a hundred weddings where he'd come home and some guest he'd picked up had proposed to him.

Cassie wanted to cry. She wanted to throw things. How come it was so easy for other women to find love? "She didn't throw the bouquet."

"What?" Once again he looked as though she might be speaking a language other than English.

"Throwing the bouquet? It's a tradition at weddings. The single women all gather and the bride throws her bouquet. Whoever catches it is, according to tradition, the next one who will get married."

His eyes narrowed in suspicion, or maybe fear. "Yeah, so?"

"So I know Serena, she'd have thrown her bouquet right into my arms. I told her if I agreed to be a bridesmaid she had to promise not to throw the bouquet."

"Totally not getting this."

"Think about it. Imagine Serena threw her bouquet right at me and I caught it. What would all the wedding guests do? What would your sandbox buddies do?"

"They'd give me a hard time, I guess."

"They'd start hinting and joking that you and I were next. I didn't want to push you into something you didn't want to do."

"You're pushing me now."

"No. I'm being honest now. There's a difference."

"There's no need to shout."

"You started it."

He took a deep breath, a breath so deep it puffed out those world-famous abs. The ones she'd run her tongue over so many times. "We're both tired. Let's go to bed and we'll talk in the morning."

"Are you going to change your mind?"

"About what?"

"Are you suddenly, in the space of eight hours, going to realize you return my feelings?"

"Cassie…" She could see he was wretched. He felt bad, of course he did—it must be mortifying to have to say no to a woman who was offering her love. But his words petered out right after that tortured "Cassie…"

"I didn't think so." And she didn't think she could spend one more night with a man who couldn't love her. She was, she was beginning to realize, worth so much more. "It's probably better if you sleep at your place tonight."

"I don't want to leave you like this."

She softened. "It's not your fault. You don't love me. I'm still glad I got up my courage to tell you how I feel. I know what I want and I deserve a man who can love me, too." She reached over, took his face in her hands. "I will get over you. But I thank you for the time we've had."

"Wait, are you dumping me?"

"Hard to dump someone you've never actually dated."

"We dated."

"We've never had one single date. We've had sex."

"What about tonight? You were my date for the wedding."

"Please. You were a best man. I was a best woman. I do not recall you asking me to accompany you to this wedding." She smiled once more. She was getting sick of her own brave smiles. She wanted to crawl in bed and pull the covers over her head and wail. "It was great, very convenient for both of us, and I got carried away. That's on me. But if I let this go on, I'll only hurt more. So goodbye."

"Do you want me to finish the house?"

She shook her head. "I think I should find a contractor who is available full-time."

He stared at her as though he couldn't believe what he was hearing. Which wasn't a big surprise, since she couldn't believe she'd uttered those words. Now she'd pushed herself into her own worst nightmare. Not only did she not have Dylan, but she had no Dylan in a half-renovated house.

Way to go, Cassie.

Slowly, he got down off the barstool. He went to collect his jacket, slid it on. All the while every piece of her wanted to cling to him, to tell him she'd changed her mind, he could stay, work on her house when he had nothing better to do, anything.

But from somewhere she found the strength, or the stubborn pride, to let him gather his things.

At last he came over and put his arms around her. "I hope you get everything you want."

She hugged him back. "You, too."

After he left, she went to find the cat. She needed the comfort of one creature on the earth who loved her absolutely.

22

"OVER HERE," DYLAN yelled, his skates racing across the ice. "I'm open."

Normally Adam was their top scorer, but today Dylan was a man with a mission. The cool thing about having played hockey with Max and Adam since they were in grade school was that they knew each other so well. With the kind of telepathic communication they seemed to have on the ice, the trio changed their usual strategy. Instead of feeding Adam the puck, they started setting Dylan up.

And he came through. Driven by a kind of fury.

He was unstoppable, everywhere at once. Adam and Max could barely keep up with him on the front line.

Inevitably, they won their game against the Preoria Pirates by a wide margin.

"Somebody took their badass vitamins this morning," Adam panted as they made their way to the dressing room.

"You're getting soft. It's all that newlywed sex. Bad for your game."

Dylan headed straight for the shower, scrubbing his scalp hard. When he came out, Max handed him a beer.

He sat down on a bench, his towel wrapped around his waist.

Adam pointed at his midsection. "Heard you went viral."

He could pretend not to understand what Adam was talking about, but these two knew him too well. The guys at the station had ribbed him unmercifully on his first day back. His new nickname was Betty, for Betty Grable. Or maybe Bettie Page. He patted his abs. "Thinking of getting the six-pack insured," he told them. "For when Hollywood comes calling."

After he dodged a glove sailing at him from one bench and a smelly kneepad coming from the other direction, he took a long swig of cold beer. "How's married life?" he asked Adam.

"Sweet."

"Good. You picked a honeymoon destination yet?" Adam and Serena weren't taking a honeymoon until after Badges on Ice, which was a good thing, seeing as Adam was their center forward and this was the year the Hunter Hurricanes were going to bag the league championship if they kept playing the way they had been.

"She wants to go to Italy."

"Nice."

"We'll do a cycling tour, rent a villa, relax."

He waited for the usual feeling of relief to wash over him, that no woman expected him to ride along beside her in a foreign country on a bicycle or to hang out in a villa, but instead he experienced a feeling of loss. Almost of envy.

Which was crazy and disturbing. He wasn't anywhere near ready to settle down. He was in his prime. One day, sure, he'd spend a couple of weeks in Hawaii with the new Mrs. Cross, but that wouldn't be happening for a while. And everyone had better get on board with the program.

"How are your wedding plans coming?" Adam asked Max.

What were they? A bunch of girls drinking tea?

Max didn't seem to find the question unmanly. But then, he was from South America, so what did he know?

"We're getting married in Alaska. As far as I know, Claire's grandmother and her friend who manages a hotel are organizing the whole thing. All we have to do is show up."

Adam nodded. Dylan waited for him to ask about the flower arrangements, but instead he said, "Did she get back okay?"

"Yep. I miss her like crazy. Think I'll fly up myself next week. I'll make sure I'm back in time for Badges on Ice."

"You'd better be," Dylan warned.

"Bring Claire," Adam added.

"How's Cassie's house coming?" Adam asked after another minute.

The grinding sense of injustice he'd felt since he left her place after the wedding made him scowl. "I wouldn't know. She fired me."

"What?" both men said at once.

Then, at the same time, "What did you do?" and "Did you screw up?" echoed in his ears.

"I didn't do anything. And no, I didn't screw up, okay? I got my real job back. I'm a firefighter again."

"That's great that you got your job back," Adam said, giving him the cop look, the one that probably made innocent men admit to crimes they'd never committed. "But why did she fire you?"

"Because I'm not available twenty-four-seven to finish her house. She's hiring somebody who is."

"Doesn't sound like Cassie."

Max shook his head in silent agreement.

"Well, that's what she did. She fired my ass."

"Who'd she get in your place?"

"I don't know. We're not exactly hanging out these days."

"So you did screw up."

Max nodded, as though he'd put the facts through his computer brain and come up with a definitive equation. "He screwed up."

"Look, it's personal." He was not going to announce that Cassie wanted more from the relationship than he had to give any more than he was going to ask Max what kind of icing was going to be on the wedding cake.

At least one man in this shower room still had his balls intact, and he intended to keep it that way.

"MAYBE I SHOULD sell it," Cassie said, looking around her. The house renovation hadn't moved forward much since she'd told Dylan she no longer needed his services. She was trying. Going to demonstrations at Home Depot on setting tile and watching YouTube videos on how to install crown molding. But apart from the fact that what seemed simple in a hardware-store demo, or in a video, was never simple when she actually tried to do it, she didn't want to renovate her house all by herself.

"You can't sell your house," Serena exclaimed. "You love it."

"Not anymore. I see him everywhere. Every time I look at the kitchen counter I remember how we—" She cleared her throat.

Serena smiled reminiscently. "We christened ours, too. That was a fun day in home renovation."

"Except that you still have Adam, and all I have is cold stone and memories I'd rather forget."

"We'll find you another contractor."

"I don't want another contractor." She knew she was whining but she didn't care. "How come you and Claire can find such good guys, and I go and fall for the Last Bachelor Standing?"

"I don't know how well he's standing," Serena said after a moment. "I think he's hurting, too."

"Good. He broke my heart."

"I know."

"I was fine until he showed up."

"I know."

She scowled even deeper. "This is all Adam's fault."

"I know."

Cassie had to chuckle at her own foolishness and Serena's patient answers. "Of course it's not Adam's fault. He tried to do me a good deed."

"Well, don't think he's happy. He told me to tell you that as soon as he finishes installing the new windows in our place, he's all yours. He feels terrible the way things turned out. We both do."

"I'll be okay. I need to get past this. And I will." Maybe. Or maybe she would finish the reno with a view to selling. Why not? According to those renovation shows she could no longer bear to watch because there was no one to make foolish bets with, she'd likely increased the value of this home. She could sell, find something else. Start again.

And her next contractor would either be female or a happily married guy with a beer belly and a house full of kids.

Twinkle was hanging around her constantly. She knew the cat missed Dylan. Who didn't?

She stroked the cat's belly. "Maybe I made a mistake."

"Of course you didn't. It's a great house."

"No, I mean dumping Dylan. Maybe I should have— I don't know, kept sleeping with him. At least I'd have a piece of him."

"You really love him."

What was the point in denial? She nodded. Miserable.

"I think you did the right thing. Nobody wants half a man." Serena put her hands out. "Even if it's half of Dylan. It would be okay if you were both only interested in having some fun, but once you fell in love with him, there was no way you could be casual."

"Exactly."

She stopped stroking the cat and it bumped her hand with its head in protest. She went back to her task. To Serena, she said, "Shouldn't you be with Adam? You two are newlyweds."

"He's playing hockey. They're playing one of their last games before the big tournament."

"Oh." She did not want to picture Dylan on the ice, bashing a hockey puck around with the other overgrown boys.

"Cassie." Serena pulled up her appointment calendar. Which was kind of like a superhero pulling on their cape or picking up their special tool. "I'm freeing Adam up. You can have him next weekend and he'll finish the rooms that are half-done. Then, maybe when you've had some time, you can figure out how you want to tackle the rest."

"No." Cassie realized she did have one more option.

"I have a good contractor who will drop everything and be here in a couple of days."

"Is he reliable?" A frown creased Serena's brow.

"The best."

"Did you find him on Craigslist? Because you know some of those guys—"

"It's my dad. He's been dying to come up and take over and I was so determined to do this all my way that I told him I'd call him if I needed him." She let out a breath and sat up, realizing it was time to end her pity party. "It's time to call him."

DYLAN SHOULD BE on top of the world. The happiest guy in Hunter, if not Washington State. Maybe the entire lower forty-eight. He had his job back, and it was the job he'd been born to do.

Ever since he'd gone home and realized how much he'd bought into a version of heroism that wasn't even true, he'd felt calmer. Throwing himself into harm's way was never going to bring his father back, and rushing into danger without a second thought was pure foolishness. He hoped he'd always go to the limit of his endurance to save a fellow human being from fire, automobile wreck or whatever disaster he was called out to, but he also hoped he'd be able to distinguish the sensible risk from the foolish one.

He'd had a long talk with his captain after dinner at the fire hall. They'd sat over coffee and Len had suddenly said, "Do you know the serenity prayer?"

"The one from AA?"

"That very one."

"God grant me—wisdom? Patience? It's something like that."

"It's the first part that everyone remembers. 'God

grant me the serenity to accept the things I cannot change, courage to change the things I can and the wisdom to know the difference.'" He leaned forward. "That's your job. You've got more courage than most men I know, but you need to figure out the serenity and wisdom parts."

Dylan nodded. He finally got it. "I feel like something changed inside me. I'm not blowing smoke, I really do. But it's still going to be a test every time."

"One day at a time. That's part of the prayer, too."

"You seem to know that prayer pretty well."

"Been going faithfully to AA meetings every week for the past thirty years. We all have our demons, Dylan. The strong man figures out what they are and learns to manage them."

He nodded. Humbled that the man he admired so much would take him into his confidence like this. "One day at a time."

"That's right. One day at a time. It's the same for all of us."

Besides having his job back and a new perspective on himself, his hockey team was poised to win the Badges on Ice championship. Adam had fought down his own personal demons with the help of some excellent performance coaching from the delectable Serena. Max was the kind of guy who always played at the top of his game—it's how he was built. And the rest of the team was solid. Even if they didn't win, they'd never played better or had more fun as a team.

But Dylan wasn't the happiest man in the lower forty-eight. He wasn't even the happiest man on his block. He woke in the night reaching for a warm, willing woman who wasn't there. He came up with a better plan for the layout of Cassie's en suite, but he wasn't the guy fixing up her house anymore. It wasn't his business.

She'd told him she loved him. Why did she have to say those fateful words? Why couldn't she have left things as they were?

And why did he have to miss her so much?

23

After a particularly eventful day of washing the fire trucks and appearing at the local high school as part of a community-awareness program, Dylan made a detour on his way home. He'd drawn up his ideas for Cassie's en suite. If she was there, he'd give it to her. If not, he'd put the drawing in the mailbox. Of course, he knew from the time of day that there was a pretty good chance she'd be home.

He felt his heart rate speed up a little as he headed down her road. He pulled into the drive, wishing he'd thought this through a little better. What was he going to say if she did open the door?

He turned off the truck and jumped down, the sketch in his hand. As he headed for the door he was intercepted by the cat. She was more like a dog, from what he could tell—she knew the sound of his truck and ran to greet him. At the last minute, she seemed to remember she was a feline and that he hadn't been around too much lately, for she stuck her tail straight up in the air and stalked past him before reversing direction and butting up against his legs.

He knelt right down, hadn't realized how much he

missed the little girl. "Hey, Twinkle. You're getting so big." He lifted the cat onto his shoulder for the comforting sound of the warm, purring creature. Cassie was a lot less likely to throw something at him if he was holding her cat.

He knocked on the door, trying to rehearse what he was going to say and realizing he didn't have a clue.

Just as well because when the door opened, it wasn't Cassie standing there. It was an older guy with gray hair and a suntan wearing an old pair of jeans and a sweatshirt from the 1984 Olympic Games in L.A. It would have been a collector's item if it wasn't so stained and faded.

"Help you?" the older guy said.

"Are you the new contractor?"

"Yep."

"I'm the old one."

The old guy looked less than impressed. "The one she fired."

"Uh, is Cassie here?"

For a second he thought the door was going to slam in his face, but then a reprieve came in the form of a comfortable woman, as tanned as the contractor but a lot better dressed. And friendlier.

"I thought I heard the door." She looked him up and down with no attempt at subtlety. "We're Cassie's parents, and you are—"

"I'm Dylan Cross, ma'am. It's a pleasure to meet you." He reached out and shook her hand. Then held his hand out to Cassie's dad, who shook it briefly before saying to his wife, "This is the guy Cassie fired."

Cassie's mom smiled. "Don't mind him. He's in a bad mood. He had to cut one piece of molding three times before he got it right."

Dad glared at both of them before stomping off into the interior of the house. The bump of feet on steps told Dylan, who knew the sounds of this house as well as he knew his own, that Dad was headed down to the basement. Hopefully not to load his rifle.

"Is Cassie here? I have something for her."

Cassie's mom hollered up the stairs, in true mom fashion, "Cassie, honey, there's somebody at the door to see you."

"Who is it?"

"Come down and see for yourself."

He heard scuffling and then the sound of her feet running down the stairs. She saw him and stopped. Her cheeks pinkened and her mouth opened in surprise. "Dylan."

Looking up at her made everything click into place somehow. "Hi," he said, feeling like a fool standing there while Cassie's mother looked on.

"Hi."

She came down the rest of the way. "What are you doing here?"

Seriously, did the mother not have anything better to do than stand here and listen to every word?

"I brought you something."

"What?"

He offered her the paper with the sketch on it. "I was thinking about the upstairs bathroom, your en suite. If you went with a smaller vanity, there's room for a good-size cupboard for towels and things."

She glanced at the paper and back at him. "Thanks. I'll give it to my dad. He and Mom came up from California to help me finish the house renovation."

She seemed as though she was waiting for him to leave, but he couldn't go. He couldn't walk away again.

"Could I talk to you outside?"

She looked as if she might refuse. Stuck her hands in the pockets of her jeans. Then she nodded. Once. "Sure."

He opened the door and held it for her, happy that Mom didn't follow them out. Though he wouldn't put it past her to peek at them out of the window.

When they got outside, he didn't know what to say. She appeared tired, as though maybe she hadn't been sleeping any better than he had. "I miss you," he said, which wasn't at all what he'd intended.

She made a sad face. "I miss you, too."

"Look, I can't give you what you want right now, but it doesn't mean I never will. Can't we get back together and see where this goes? What's the rush?"

"There's no rush. But you don't want what I want, and it hurts me too much to hang around hoping you'll suddenly love me." He could barely hear her with the damn cat purring so loudly in his ear.

He scowled, feeling that he'd somehow been led astray and not knowing how or when it had happened. "Everything was great until the day Adam and Serena got married. And then it's like you flipped into bride mode. All I'm asking for is time."

Once more she looked at him sadly. "See, I've done this before. Waited around for a guy to realize that he cares for me. In fact, I've been right where you are before, too. You think this is okay. It's better than being alone, and who knows, maybe one day I'll realize that this person really is the love of my life. But the truth is, you know it or you don't. I think you might be it for me. And I'm not it for you. So it's not your fault and it's not my fault, but I deserve better than to have the man I love hanging around trying to decide if he wants more."

"You're not being fair."

"Maybe not. But I'm thirty years old. I've got a house, a biological clock." She glanced at the vibrating fur ball on his shoulder. "And I've got a cat. All I need now is the right man."

It had been bad enough having the door to her home opened by another contractor, even if the dude had turned out to be her dad, but to have another man in her bed? Another man putting kids in her nursery? In a second of blinding clarity he realized there was only one man who was going to do those things. And he was that man.

"No," he said.

"No?"

"No. You're not putting another man in my place. I've put a lot of myself into that house."

She raised an eyebrow.

"And this cat is crazy about me."

She glanced at the cat with something like pity. "Lots of females are crazy about you. We can't help it. You're like catnip."

His jaw fell open. "Did you just compare me to a weed?"

"I believe I did."

"Well, this chunk of catnip has taken root in your garden and it is not going to be dug out." What in the hell was he talking about?

Her lips twitched but her eyes remained serious. "What are you trying to say, Dylan?"

"I love you." Once more, words seemed to come out of his mouth that he didn't remember forming in his brain and sending down the appropriate neural pathways. They seemed to form randomly and leap out.

And yet, exactly like when she'd walked down the

stairs and he'd felt something click into place, as he told her he loved her, he realized it was true. He hadn't planned it, didn't even notice it was happening while he'd been falling, but fall he had. And hard.

He felt a smile start to split his face. "I love you."

She wasn't throwing her arms around him and inviting him home for dinner with the folks. She narrowed her eyes. "I don't believe you."

"It's true. I have never said those words to another woman. Except my mom. And then only on Mother's Day and her birthday. I don't go throwing around *I love you*s like they're nothing."

"I don't think so."

"It's true. How can I prove it to you?"

"You don't have to prove you love someone."

But, he thought, sometimes when you'd hurt someone and you didn't mean to, then maybe you did need to prove it.

He simply needed to figure out how.

He handed her back the kitten, then kissed her hard. "I'll be back. Don't you even think about dating anyone else."

"I—"

He yanked open the door of his truck. "Oh, and don't let your dad touch the en suite."

"He came here to help finish the renos."

"He had to cut one piece of molding three times before he got it right. Your mom told me. He is not touching that bathroom."

"You have no right to—"

He walked back to her, pulled her to him and kissed her while she was still talking. He smiled down at the outrage on two female faces glaring at him.

24

"IT'S A FOUR-HOUR drive to the rink where Badges on Ice is being held, so we should carpool," Max said, as they headed for the ice and their last practice before the big tournament. Max was always the one thinking ahead about things like logistics.

Dylan rubbed an itchy spot where his wool sock rubbed, right under his knee. "Sure, whatever."

"We can meet right here at the practice rink. It's central for all of us and then we can all go in one vehicle."

It was exactly what they'd done last year, so Dylan wasn't sure why they were having a discussion. They'd all piled into his truck last year. The backseat was a little cramped, but Max was shorter than Dylan and Adam, so he hadn't complained. They'd thrown all the hockey equipment in the truck bed and they were good to go.

Adam must have wondered the same thing, but Max didn't start a conversation without a reason.

"I'm wondering if we should take two vehicles. I can't see how we're going to fit five adults and all our equipment into one of our current rides."

Five people? Then it hit him. Max was taking Claire

and Serena was going along to cheer her new husband. He was the fifth wheel.

"I'll take my own truck," he said. "We can throw all the equipment in the back. You can put four adults in Adam's Jeep." Since Max had one of those stupid billionaire sports cars.

"We should travel together," Adam argued. Half the fun last year had been the joking around on the way down. But even if they could all cram into one vehicle, the ride was never going to be the same with two women along. They might as well accept that things had changed.

"I'll want my own wheels. When we win, we'll be heroes. I might get lucky with some hot groupie. Wouldn't want you guys cramping my style." He tried to exude excitement at this prospect, but really all he felt was a dull ache when he thought about hooking up with anyone but Cassie.

Both of the other men nodded, and Adam said, "Sure," but he was pretty certain they could see right through his bravado to the pain of loss.

She wasn't taking his calls. Ever since he'd dropped off that sketch, she'd ignored his calls and texts. Okay, you didn't have to be a genius to see she didn't want to talk to him. Fine. He'd never in his life gone crawling back to a woman with his tail between his legs. Why the hell was this one different?

Twinkle did not love Cassie's parents. She wasn't sure why, since they were perfectly nice people who liked animals. But the cat would either jump into Cassie's lap and loudly demand attention or stalk out of the room, tail in the air, stiff with displeasure whenever they were around. It was her mother who diagnosed the problem. "She's jealous."

The strange thing was, the cat hadn't been a bit jealous of Dylan when he was around. If anything, Cassie thought Twinkle associated the arrival of her mom and dad with the disappearance of her hero.

Well, the kitten might as well learn the bitter truth while she was young enough to recover. Guys like Dylan were great when they were around, fun and sexy and excellent to look at. But don't count on them for the long term.

She knew she wasn't being entirely reasonable. Was he really supposed to delay his return to his job because he'd committed to her and her house? Was it his fault he couldn't return her love? But disappointment and the crushing humiliation of having told a man she loved him and seeing his eyes look wild with panic had soured her on reason.

She'd loved. She'd lost. She hurt.

Her parents had taken the day off to visit some old friends in the area. She had a feeling her dad might also be suffering a little hurt pride. She hadn't let him touch her upstairs bathroom. And not because he'd cut one piece of molding three times—though she could see that his work wasn't quite the professional standard of Dylan's—but because some foolish flicker of hope still insisted on burning within her.

She noticed that Twinkle hadn't touched the food she'd put out this morning, very un-Twinkle-like behavior. You could pretty much set your clock to Twinkle's inner dinner gong. "Twinkle?" she called, looking in all the cat's favorite spots around the house. But the kitten wasn't sleeping on the window seat in her bedroom, or in the rocking chair in the spare room, or the one chair she allowed her in the living room.

She wasn't curled on the warmest spot on the heated tiles on the bathroom floor.

Cassie headed outside at last. "Twinkle?"

A sad and mournful meow filtered down through the branches of the cedar tree in the backyard.

She walked under it and looked up. Way up. She had a moment of déjà vu when she recalled Dylan climbing down this same tree with the kitten that first day.

"Oh, come on. You know how to climb down from there."

The piteous cry she received in return suggested that she was mistaken. And indeed, it did seem as though the little cat had gone a lot higher than ever before.

She went back into the kitchen and fetched the dish of cat food and took it out, standing under the branches where the cat could see it. "Look, here's your favorite kibble. Mmm. Tuna. Come on."

Nothing could have been more heartrending than the sound that traveled down to her. She saw the cat make a tentative move, and then it seemed to tumble with a screech, claws digging into rough bark. Cassie's heart felt as though it was caught in her throat as she watched the bundle of fur skid down and finally come to rest in a V of branches. She thought she might be more scared than the cat as she put the food down.

If only Dylan was here. But Dylan wasn't here and, like fixing up the house, she was going to have to add rescuing cats out of trees to the list of her responsibilities. "Well," she said to the cat, "I helped rescue a baby whale stuck out in the ocean. I guess I can manage one small kitten in a tree."

Of course, she was a water person. She swam like

a fish, had been diving for years. Water, especially the ocean, was her natural medium. Trees, not so much.

However, she was not about to call for help, and her parents wouldn't be back for hours. She'd taken responsibility for the cat—even though she mostly blamed Dylan for that, too—so she was going to have to figure this out.

There was a ladder in the garage. She hauled it out. It was a stepladder that she'd bought to use in her painting projects. She set it up under the tree. The ground wasn't particularly even, but she moved the ladder around until she felt secure climbing up the rungs.

She got to the first thick branch and hauled herself up. Okay. So far so good. Twinkle was now much closer. Though farther up the tree than she'd realized.

Twinkle's eyes were wide and the cat stared at her as though she were her only hope.

Cassie felt the stickiness of sap on the next branch as she gingerly pulled herself up. The smell of cedar was strong. If she didn't look down it wasn't too bad. She took a breath. Rose shakily, scraping her knee on tree bark as she did so. There were cedar fronds tangling in her hair and bits of greenery were dropping on her.

Her stomach felt the way it used to when she got onto a roller coaster, or one of the wild and scary rides at the fair, right before the ride began, when the bar was locked in place and it was too late to change her mind, a kind of excitement tinged with fear. Or more likely fear tinged with excitement.

She breathed in and out slowly. A diver learned to control her breathing or risk disaster. She felt the principle must be the same on land.

Something about the way that cat was staring at her gave her the courage to go on. It was only a tree, for goodness' sake. She'd dived shipwrecks under the ocean, sailed through storms that chucked heavy waves over the bows and tossed the ship around like a cork in a washing machine. This was a giant evergreen rooted to the earth. She'd be fine.

She pulled and hauled herself up to the next branch. She could see that strategy would be needed to get the rest of the way. She had to pick a route with well-spaced branches. At one point, Twinkle put out a paw and batted the air as though encouraging her progress.

"Hang on," she said. Probably to both of them. "I'm coming."

She heard a car go by and was shocked at how far below her the rumble of the engine sounded.

But she was close now, too close to give up. "Almost there," she assured Twinkle, who meowed helplessly in response.

The branches were getting skinnier, so she tested each one thoroughly before putting her full weight on it. Finally, she got within reaching distance of the cat.

"There you go," she crooned. "There's my girl."

Until this moment she hadn't realized how much she'd come to love this small creature who'd adopted her. The fur was soft against her face as she lifted Twinkle into her arms. She thought they were both trembling, or maybe that was only her trembling enough for both of them.

She gave them both a minute, then said, "Okay. Now all we have to do is get back down." With a lot more confidence than she felt, because the thing about that famous advice not to look down was that it only worked when you're climbing up something. It was impossible to climb down a tree and not look in that direction.

Which was paralyzing.

How had the ground slipped so far beneath her?

And how had it not occurred to her that climbing up unencumbered was a lot easier than climbing down with a terrified kitten in tow?

25

"Okay, that's the last of it," Max said as the final hockey bag thumped into the back of Dylan's truck.

The two couples were driving together in Adam's Jeep since Max's Tesla only seated two.

"Are you sure we can't all fit in one vehicle?" Serena said, seeming uncertain.

"Can't fit all five of us and the luggage in one," Max reminded her.

Serena, however, was both intuitive and tenacious. She said, "Well, why don't we girls drive down together in your fancy sports car? And you boys can travel together."

Claire agreed, but it was Dylan who refused the change of plan. And suddenly, he exploded. "Damn it, she should be here."

No one had to ask him which *she* he was referring to.

"I agree," Serena said. "She should."

"Well, it's too late now," Adam said. "We're locked and loaded."

"You go on ahead," Dylan said. "I'll call her again." And if she didn't answer, he figured he'd drive by her house. Badges on Ice was a big deal to him, to Adam and to Max. They both had their women by their sides. He wanted his woman, wanted her so badly he felt as though part of him was missing.

Adam sent him a level look. "You've got all our stuff. Could you maybe kiss and make up after the weekend?"

"No."

His old buddy shook his head. "Don't screw this up."

But Serena walked up to him, Claire right behind her. "Don't let her go."

"I don't plan to."

"You need some performance coaching?"

He was about to say no and make a joke, but he realized he needed all the help he could get, and this woman was brilliant at what she did. Plus, she was friends with Cassie, so that had to be a bonus.

"Honey, we don't have time," Adam said, with barely controlled impatience.

"We built extra time into the schedule," she said with unruffled calm. "We can spare a few minutes."

She didn't bother reminding Adam that they only had this shot at winning because she'd coached the man who was now her husband out of his fear of success, helped him slay his demons. And it was Max and Dylan who'd talked him into letting her help him.

Adam obviously picked up the unspoken messages, because he said, "Ten minutes, tops." And he and Max walked out of hearing range. For which Dylan was profoundly grateful.

Claire touched his arm. "Good luck. You two belong together." And then she walked to join her husband-to-be and Adam getting cold drinks from the vending machine outside the rink.

There was a grassy area and a couple of picnic tables, part of the park that housed the rink. Serena led them there and sat down, motioning him to sit opposite. "Tell me what's going on," she said.

Dylan wanted to tell Serena about his personal failings about as much as he wanted to stop a puck with his face. But he wanted Cassie. So he told Serena about how he and Cassie had started out having so much fun, how the relationship had sneaked into something different when he wasn't paying attention.

Serena didn't interrupt or give him withering looks. She paid attention, nodding once in a while, her gaze steady on his face. "Then she told me she loved me and I panicked. I'd got my job back and figured out why I was acting like such a hothead, because I was trying to become the man my father was. The one everybody in my family worships. But to become a dead hero, you have to die first. Which is pretty much what I was trying to do."

"That's an amazing piece of self-discovery. Good work." She sounded genuinely impressed. He'd been so busy beating himself up for letting Cassie down that it was nice to take a moment and realize that he was making progress as a human being.

"Thanks."

"It sounds like it was a lot to take in all at once, a big personal revelation, getting your job back and then having Cassie share her feelings."

Her words suddenly made him feel uncomfortable. "It was, but that doesn't mean I didn't want to hear them. I— Maybe I fell back into my old pattern with women."

"What pattern is that?"

This introspection stuff was pretty new to him, but he'd been wondering if his rashness at work was related to his inability to commit. If anyone could help him figure it out, she was sitting across from him. "Maybe I didn't want my wife to spend her life staring at a photograph in the living room. Maybe I didn't want my kids growing up with no father."

She smiled at him, sort of like a teacher about to give a kid a colored sticker for getting the answer to a tough question. "If you push women away, you'll never have to worry about leaving a widow or fatherless children."

He nodded, feeling a lot clearer for giving his thoughts voice.

She said, "Firefighting is still a dangerous profession. You could be killed or injured."

"I know." He shifted on the hard bench.

"But firefighters get married all the time. They have kids."

"They do."

"Do you think, now that you're not aiming at being a dead hero, that you might have more to offer a woman than a photograph on the mantel?"

He took a deep breath. "I do."

"Then all you have to do is convince her."

"But how?"

"Try telling her what you've told me. Tell her you love her."

As she rose and motioned to the others, who were watching from across the tarmac, he pulled out his phone.

He didn't expect Cassie to answer, was all set to tell her on voice mail that he loved her and he was on his way to pick her up for the big game. But to his surprise, she answered right away.

"D-Dylan?"

At that one word, everything he'd been planning to say dropped away. He knew the sound of fear. He was already on his feet, heading for his truck. "What's wrong?"

There was a sound of rustling. Then a puff of suppressed air like a sigh escaping. "I'm stuck in a tree."

"What?"

"I climbed up to get Twinkle, who climbed too high and couldn't get down. And now we're both stuck."

"Don't move. I'm on my way."

"And Dylan?"

"Yeah?" He was jamming keys into the ignition.

"Don't you dare tell anyone."

"Never. Hang on tight."

His tires squealed as he roared out of the drive, past four startled faces. No time to explain. He took the shortcuts he'd come to know, going as fast as he dared down residential streets on a Saturday.

The truck jerked to a stop in her drive as he jammed on the brakes. He was out the door and sprinting around the house. It might sound funny for a grown woman to get stuck in a tree, but all he could think about was her falling. The fear was like a painful vise around his chest.

He approached the tree cautiously. The stepladder was out, so no need to figure out which tree. He looked up. She was hanging on, half sitting, her weight supported on a nice thick branch. He saw instantly what had happened. The branch below her had snapped under her weight. She'd done the sensible thing and stayed where she was.

Twinkle gave an almighty howl when she saw Dylan. Which made Cassie look down. "Oh, thank God," she said when she saw him.

He gave her his most reassuring smile. "You stay right where you are. I'm on my way."

He was up that tree in no time, keeping up a cheerful monologue designed to keep both his girls calm. When he reached them, he said, "Okay. Here's how we're going to do this. I'll take the cat." That was easy, since she scrambled into his arms, as though figuring out that he was the easiest ticket out of there.

"The branch broke," Cassie said. "I was doing fine, but the branch broke."

"I saw. Now that you don't have the cat, I think it will be easier." He held out one hand. "Put your right foot into my hand."

She moved herself around until she could.

"Good. Now hang on to your branch and I'll ease your foot down to a solid hold. When I tell you, you can put your weight on it, got it?"

"Yeah."

Branch by branch, he got them down. When Cassie made it to the last stage, dropping down into his arms, he held on, looked down into her face and kissed her.

"Thank you," she said breathlessly.

The cat was already chowing down on the dish of food sitting at the bottom of the tree.

"Why didn't you call me?" he asked. He couldn't believe she'd been stuck up there and hadn't called for help.

"I was trying to get down on my own."

He got it. "Sort of thing I'd do," he admitted. His heart was still beating uncomfortably fast. Not for himself, he could climb up and down trees all day, but the thought of her slipping and getting hurt had terrified him.

"I've got some things I need to say to you," he said. "But maybe I should make you some tea or something."

"There's lemonade in the fridge."

The cat followed them in, winding around his legs and making a fuss until he picked her up.

"You have not been practicing those lessons on tree climbing I gave you," he said sternly.

The cat flipped over, offering her belly.

"Do not give me the adorable face. You're going to have to pay attention in the future." The cat began to purr.

CASSIE FELT FOOLISH, irritated and so glad to see Dylan that her teeth hurt.

After she got the lemonade out of the fridge and pulled down two glasses, she turned to find he'd put the cat down and was standing behind her grinning. "What's so funny?" she demanded.

"I was thinking how Adam saved Serena from a psycho killer, and Max and Claire survived a plane crash in a sabotaged aircraft, and I was feeling like I wasn't in the same league. But I am. I saved your life today."

He'd helped her climb down from a tree. Technically, she wasn't sure it was in the same category as crashing planes and serial killers, but she didn't feel like being too nitpicky. A rescue was a rescue.

"I told you I was going to prove to you that I love you."

There were those words. Those magic words she'd longed to hear. But seriously? He thought this was proof? "There was no way you could have predicted Twinkle would get stuck in the tree again. Besides, you're a firefighter. Rescuing cats out of trees is what you do."

"And women. I rescued a woman, too."

"And women."

"That's not the proof."

She put her hands on her hips. "Oh? And what is?"

He reached for the hem of his T-shirt and pulled it over his head. Bits of tree flew off as he pulled the material from his body. And then he revealed those abs that she hadn't seen in far too long, the abs that women all over the world had been downloading like crazy, and because she was sidetracked by the image of Mr. June, which was so much more in person, he had to clear his throat to get her to stop staring at his stomach.

He'd raised his arms. With his left hand he pointed to the tattoo circling his right bicep. With his arms raised she could see the colored links of the people he loved. But something looked different. One of them seemed brighter red. She stepped closer, her heart racing faster than the cat was purring at their feet.

He'd added another link. It was the letter *C*. In red. If she'd wanted proof, she supposed she had it. Her initial inked into his skin.

"Oh, Dylan."

"You're going to have to marry me now. I tattooed you on my arm."

She stepped closer, putting a fingertip beneath the new link. Marriage? He was talking marriage?

"If you say no, I'll be doomed to only dating Christines and Charmaines and women named Carol. And I don't want any of them. I only want—"

She kissed him, going up on tiptoes to reach his foolish mouth. And he put his arms around her and kissed her back. When they came up for air, he said, "There's so much I need to say to you, but right now, I only need you to believe that I love you and will for the rest of my life."

"You know, FYI, an engagement ring presented on bended knee would have done the trick."

He scoffed. "Any fool can run to a jeweler and pick out a sparkly ring. But a tattoo? That's commitment. What more do you want?"

"A date would be nice."

"A date?" He looked totally confused.

"Do you realize we've never had a single date?"

He nodded with great seriousness. "I will take you on a date. Today."

She threw her arms around his neck and said, "You did save my life." She kissed him, a big smacking kiss on the mouth. "Just like I saved yours."

She leaned into him, smelling the warmth of his skin, longing to have him back in her bed. "You know, my folks will be home soon. I can't wait to tell them the good news."

"Text them. We've got to get going."

"What? Where?"

"Badges on Ice. Grab a toothbrush."

"Wait, I can't possibly—"

"You agreed to go on a date with me. Today."

"That's your idea of our first date? Watching you play hockey?" She was almost too shocked to laugh. The man was certifiable.

"Cassie? Commitment goes both ways. Badges on Ice is extremely important to me. That's why I called you. The others are heading to the game, but I couldn't leave without you. It wasn't right."

Maybe not history's most romantic speech, but she understood the subtext. "Fine. I'll grab a toothbrush and some clean clothes."

He rubbed a hand over his new tattoo as though maybe it itched.

"Oh, and just so you know, there is no way I am getting your name tattooed on my flesh."

"You've got five minutes to pack. We'll design your tattoo in the truck on the way to the game."

She ran upstairs and into her bathroom, the one he was going to turn into something magical. He'd figured out how to steal some space from the third bedroom that you'd hardly notice. Not only enough to put in a linen closet, but to put in a nice steam shower with plenty of room for two.

"Can you grab me some jeans and a clean shirt out of my dresser?" she yelled from the bathroom.

"Can do."

He found an overnight bag in her closet and grabbed some lacy underwear, a couple of shirts, jeans. Socks. He found a nightshirt that he particularly liked on her, not that she'd be wearing it much. He made a rapid search, trying to think of anything she'd need.

She came out of the bathroom with a toiletry bag.

"What's so funny?"

He kissed her. "You are." How had he almost let this woman get away? "I've figured out what you should tattoo on your body."

Her eyes narrowed. "What?"

He let out the grin he'd been trying to hold in. Held out the calendar open to June. The one he'd found hidden in her shirt drawer. "I'm thinking this would go nicely down your back."

26

"WHEN DID YOU get that tattoo?" she asked as they cruised down the highway.

"Yesterday."

"So if Twinkle didn't get stuck in the tree, when were you planning to show it to me?" Twinkle had not been happy to see the two of them leave together. Cassie had left a note for her parents, who, come to think of it, wouldn't be too pleased, either.

"When I got up the nerve."

"But I told you I love you. You had to know I was a sure thing."

"You had me scared."

"Well, you hurt me."

He reached over and grabbed her hand. "I know. And I'm sorry."

She watched the trees flash by as they rolled down the highway. Dark green evergreens like the one she'd recently been stuck in. She hadn't had time for a shower. She had a terrible feeling she smelled like one of those air fresheners shaped like a tree. "My dad's upset."

"He barely knows me."

"I wouldn't let him start work on the upstairs bathroom. I guess I did believe you were coming back."

When he told her about the thinking he'd been doing and the conclusions he'd come to, she could see that the time away from her had been good for him.

"It was Serena who finally convinced me that I should come after you today."

"And I am grateful to her. On many levels." How long would she have stayed up that tree before she caved and called somebody?

She glanced at him, smiling. "I'm glad it was you who rescued me."

"Me, too."

More miles went by. Traffic crawled almost to a standstill and she began to worry, but Dylan grabbed her hand and told her not to. "We'll get there or we won't. There's no point fretting."

This was Dylan? The guy who lived for hockey?

While they were nearly stopped, he asked, "How's your whale?"

"Not my whale. But thanks for asking. He's back with his pod." And that was one of the happiest endings she'd ever seen.

"I'm glad. Every lonely male needs a family."

She leaned over so she could kiss him. "Yes, they do."

"You made it," Adam said, looking harassed, when they got to the hotel where they'd all spend the night. "We have to leave for the arena in fifteen minutes."

"Plenty of time," Dylan said.

"I checked you in," Max said, tossing him a key. "One floor up. Two-oh-five."

"Thanks," Dylan said, sprinting to get into his uniform. Realizing Cassie wasn't following, he turned. "Cassie? I'm going to need you to unpack my stuff. We're in kind of a hurry."

"Don't even think about—what I know you're thinking about," Adam warned. Serena stepped in and spoke to Adam softly while Cassie ran after Dylan.

In the room, she found him already naked. "Come here," he said in that tone she'd missed so much.

"You have to focus on the game."

"Can't. All I can think about is you."

"But—"

"Ten minutes." He flipped down the bedcover. "Think of it as your service to the team."

"Won't you drain your energy?"

He chuckled, low and sexy. "Not hardly." And then he advanced on her and began taking off her clothes.

It was quick, and silly, and over in ten minutes, but she managed to run her tongue over the *C* on his tattoo and to enjoy a very satisfying if rushed mutual climax.

She'd spent ten minutes doing a lot less interesting things.

Dylan didn't seem drained; he seemed energized.

The guys went ahead in Dylan's truck and the women followed half an hour later in Adam's Jeep. As Serena drove, Cassie filled them in on her exciting rescue, Dylan's tattoo and his sort-of proposal.

"He never does anything in the usual fashion, does he," Serena said.

"No." And Cassie thought she could live with Dylan her whole life and never know an instant's boredom.

The rink was packed for the championship game between the Hurricanes and the Portland Paters. The men on the ice were all people who served—cops, firefighters, paramedics, some of them reserves like Max, but all dedicated to saving lives.

You'd never know it once they faced each other on the ice.

These men who regularly risked their lives to save others now seemed intent on smashing each other into the boards and scoring against their opponents at any cost.

The energy in the rink was electric. These were the serious fans. And, Cassie realized, she and Claire and Serena were three of the most serious.

They cheered themselves hoarse. Of course, only Claire remotely understood the game. Cassie and Serena simply cheered to be supportive. Sometimes they asked Claire what was going on, but mostly they simply watched their men.

The teams seemed evenly matched. There was lots of back-and-forth: Adam scored once; some huge guy from the Paters scored. Dylan scooped the puck from another player and shot from a ridiculous distance to score the second goal. It was tied up after an eye-straining number of passes leading to a brilliant shot by the Paters. At least, that's what Claire said. The score was tied two–all toward the end of the third period.

Cassie wanted them to win almost as much as she'd wanted the whale to find its way home.

"Oh, nice pass," Claire said, leaning forward. In the blur of motion, Cassie could see that Max had passed the puck to Dylan. He seemed to look at the opposing team's net, size up his opportunity.

"Don't do it," Claire muttered—she who'd been drafted to the Olympic women's hockey team. "Pass it to Adam."

It was weird—as though Dylan might have heard

her—because in another blur of motion, Cassie saw the puck fly, Adam skated hard and boom.

The puck slid past a stumbling goalie and into the net.

And it was all over. With five minutes still on the clock, all the Hurricanes had to do was play defense. And they played defense for all they were worth until the horn sounded.

The women were on their feet, screaming. "Come on," Claire said, and grabbed Cassie's hand. Cassie grabbed Serena's hand and they all ran down to the edge of the rink.

The Hurricanes were jumping at each other, hugging and banging fists. They gathered themselves for the traditional skate past where they saluted the other team.

Then the three guys skated over to where the women waited. And they all high-fived through the Plexiglas.

THE AFTER-PARTY WAS in a local bar. Everybody turned up: both teams, a bunch of the fans and a few women who didn't really even understand the rules of the game but happened to be in love with a player.

The six of them sat together enjoying hamburgers and a pitcher of beer. They talked over the game, the best moves, the near misses. At one point, Claire said, "I wasn't sure you were going to make that last pass, Dylan."

He glanced up at her, then to Serena, and finally let his gaze rest on Cassie. "I had a moment. But I'm learning that rash action isn't always the smart choice. I could have tried to be a hero and we'd have lost the game."

"By passing, you were a hero," Claire pointed out.

That was way too much serious talk for Dylan and

he immediately made a joke and then the boys were back at their teasing and insults.

Cassie figured they deserved to act like fools once in a while.

Suddenly, she could see the three as they must have been as little boys. The laughing and pushing and yet the deep bond they had with each other was evident. She'd heard that Adam's mother had some home movies of the three of them. She'd have to see if she could view those movies sometime.

Then, looking exactly like a pair of grade-school pranksters, Adam and Max suddenly got up and said, "Don't move. Be right back."

They went to a duffel bag that Max had carried in, and with their backs to the table, fished something out, then returned.

Adam stood in front of Max, shielding whatever he was currently carrying. "Dylan," he said, in a deep, mock-serious voice. "Badges on Ice isn't the only competition we three have battled for in the past year."

"No, indeed," Max intoned from behind him.

"We challenged each other at my birthday party back in February to see who would be the Last Bachelor Standing. Congratulations, Dylan. The trophy goes to you."

The Badges on Ice trophy was already sitting in the middle of their table. They'd have to give it back to have the winning team's name engraved, but for this evening, they could revel in their success. Beside the grandiose silver goblet, the trophy that was revealed when Dylan stepped aside and Max came forward was, well, on a different scale.

It looked as though they'd taken an old gold fishing trophy—with some peeled patches where the gold had rubbed off—hacked out the fish the guy in the trophy had been holding over his head and filled his two empty hands with a martini glass and a little black book. In a touch of true subtlety, they'd scribbled "Little Black Book" in gold pen on the cover of the book. They'd pasted silver duct tape over the original plaque. Now it said, "Dylan Cross. Winner. Last Bachelor Standing."

As the table erupted in applause. Dylan threw back his head and laughed. It was impossible not to join in.

Serena leaned over and said to Cassie, "I told Adam that was a terrible idea, but he didn't listen."

"It's okay."

And it was. Dylan had outlasted both his old buddies. But if she had her way, the last bachelor wouldn't be standing for long.

After the trophy had been passed around and admired by all, Dylan rose, holding the trophy aloft as though he'd won something really special.

He said, "I love a challenge. And I would love to accept this wonderful honor. But I can't."

He put the trophy down on the table, beside the much classier silver cup, and from his jacket pocket retrieved a ring box.

Cassie heard a gasp and then realized it came from her mouth. The jewelry box wasn't a new one. Cassie could see right away that the blue velvet was faded and rubbed off in patches. The laughter at their table died. They were an island of silence in the noisy bar. "Right here, in front of all of you, I want to tell you that I am in love with Cassie Price."

He flipped open the ring box before Cassie had managed to take in what was happening.

"Cassie," he said, grinning at her in the special way he had, the smile that wasn't for every woman who could afford a calendar, but that was just for her. "Will you marry me?"

Somehow, she found her voice. "Yes."

He slipped the diamond ring onto her finger. It was a tiny bit loose, but she loved the antique setting and the three diamonds in a row. It was the sort of ring that spoke of tradition and family and generations.

"It was my grandmother's ring," he told her, which she'd suspected. "I dropped by my mother's house yesterday and asked her for it." He laughed. "She's waiting by the phone right now to find out if you said yes."

Among the hugs and congratulations and maybe a few tears, she thought her future was as bright as the diamonds winking on her finger.

A couple of the younger players whom she recognized from the other team sauntered by. One of them, a young, cocky-looking guy who could have been Dylan ten years earlier, chanted, "And another one bites the dust."

Dylan wasn't at all offended. He jumped up. Clapped the younger man on the shoulder. "Hey, dude?" he said. "This is for you."

And with a swagger he presented the foolish trophy.

The young guy glanced at him and at the trophy and tucked it under his arm. "Yeah. Whatever."

"That trophy is wasted on that kid," Adam said.

"You watch," Dylan said.

Sure enough, the young buck stopped at a table of young women. Cassie couldn't see what he said, but he was obviously showing them the trophy and spinning some kind of story. Next thing she knew, he and his buddy were sitting with the table of girls.

Dylan glanced at Adam. "Not bad. One day, with practice, he'll be as smooth as me."

"Hate to break it to you, *dude,* but your smooth days are over."

"No," he said, taking Cassie's hand and kissing it. "They are only beginning."

Max filled their beer glasses from a fresh pitcher. "Everyone, raise your glasses in a toast." Everyone complied. "To Dylan and Cassie."

Naturally, some fool started banging his glass with a knife as though they were at a wedding reception, and then everyone joined in. The noise didn't stop until Dylan and Cassie leaned in and kissed each other.

"I can't believe you proposed on our first date," she said.

His trademark grin was tinged with something warm and sweet. "Wait till you see what I have planned for our second date."

* * * * *

COMING NEXT MONTH FROM

HARLEQUIN *Blaze*

Available June 17, 2014

#803 RIDING HARD
Sons of Chance • by Vicki Lewis Thompson
Large animal vet Drake Brewster might have just come to her rescue, but Tracy Gibbons knows the seemingly perfect Southern gentleman is still a no-good heartbreaker. So why can't she keep her hands off him?

#804 DOUBLE EXPOSURE
From Every Angle • by Erin McCarthy
Posing with hundreds of people wearing only body paint? Career journalist Emma Gideon agrees, just to get her story. And when she ends up in bed with rival journalist Kyle Hadley, more than just their skin is exposed....

#805 WICKED SEXY
Uniformly Hot! • by Anne Marsh
Search-and-rescue swimmer Daeg Ross is used to jumping into treacherous waters. But his feelings for relationship-shy Dani Andrews are a whole new type of risk. Together, will they sink...or swim?

#806 TAKEN BY STORM
by Heather MacAllister
When a blizzard leaves her stranded, Zoey is desperate for a way to get across the country. Luckily, a sexy and charming Texan offers her just the ride she needs....

HBCNM0614

REQUEST YOUR FREE BOOKS!
2 FREE NOVELS PLUS 2 FREE GIFTS!

HARLEQUIN

Blaze®

red-hot reads!

HB13R2

Double Exposure

by Erin McCarthy...

Emma shifted on the seat of Kyle's car, hoping she wasn't
smearing paint onto the upholstery. Why on earth had she
volunteered to do this stupid group photo shoot? With the
coworker she secretly craved, no less? The sooner she got this
paint off and some clothes on, the sooner sanity would reappear.

"Can I take a shower at your place?" Maybe properly clothed
she would be less aware of Kyle and her reaction to him. Because she could not, would not—ever—indulge herself with
Kyle. Dating and sex made people emotional and irrational.
It didn't mix with work.

"Of course you can." Kyle pulled out of the parking lot for
the short trip to his place.

She caught sight of herself in the visor mirror. She looked
worse than she'd thought. There was no way Kyle would ever

come near her like this. Her hair was shot out in all directions, and her skin was emerald-green, with the whites of her eyes and her teeth gleaming in contrast. The napkins she'd used to cover herself tufted up from her chest. "I look like a frog eating barbecue!"

Kyle started laughing so hard he ended up coughing.

"It's not funny!" she protested.

Before they could debate that, he turned in to his building. Still chuckling, he ushered her toward the stairs. "What a day." He tossed his keys onto the table inside the entry of his apartment. "Bathroom's this way. Come on."

Emma followed, her eyes inevitably drawn to his tight butt. He was muscular in an athletic, natural way. Her fingers itched to squeeze all that muscle.

"I'm really good at keeping secrets, you know." Kyle turned, his eyes dark and unreadable.

She was suddenly aware of the sexual tension between them. They were mostly naked, standing inches apart. His mouth was so close....

"If anything happens here today, you can be sure it will never be mentioned at the office."

"What could happen?" She knew what he meant, but she needed to hear confirmation that he was equally attracted to her.

"This." Kyle closed the gap between them.

Emma didn't hesitate, but let her eyes shut as his mouth covered hers in a deep, tantalizing kiss.

Pick up DOUBLE EXPOSURE by Erin McCarthy, available wherever you buy Harlequin® Blaze® books.

Saddle up for a wild ride!

Large-animal vet Drake Brewster might have just come to her rescue, but Tracy Gibbons knows the seemingly perfect Southern gentleman is still a no-good heartbreaker. So why can't she keep her hands off him?

Don't miss the latest in the
Sons of Chance trilogy

Riding Hard

from *New York Times* bestselling author

Vicki Lewis Thompson

Available July 2014, wherever you buy
Harlequin Blaze books.

Red-Hot Reads
www.Harlequin.com

HB79807

Wicked weather and wicked temptation!

Search-and-rescue swimmer Daeg Ross is used to jumping into treacherous waters. But his feelings for relationship-shy Dani Andrews are a whole new type of risk. Together, will they sink...or swim?

From the reader-favorite
Uniformly Hot! miniseries

Wicked Sexy
by *Anne Marsh*

Available July 2014, wherever you buy
Harlequin Blaze books.